"According to your file, you were the chief designer of this water feature. It's amazing."

Though her mouth remained neutral, the smile behind her eyes told him she was pleased at his compliment. "We work as a team around here. I can't take all the credit."

"You're right. But although teamwork is important, there has to be a creative lead. You're it."

When she didn't respond but instead turned her attention to clicking keys on the computer, shutting down the driving software, he chuckled and looked down at the floor, feeling heat in his neck. He wanted to give credit where credit was due, encourage an employee who needed it, but this felt more like. . . *No!*

He was *not* flirting.

ELIZABETH GODDARD is a seventh-generation Texan who recently spent five years in beautiful Southern Oregon, which serves as a setting for some of her novels. She is now back in East Texas, living near her family. When she's not writing, she's busy homeschooling her four children. Beth is the author of several novels and novellas. She's actively involved in several writing organizations including American Christian Fiction Writers (ACFW) and loves to mentor new writers.

Books by Elizabeth Goddard

HEARTSONG PRESENTS
HP777—Seasons of Love
HP893—Disarming Andi
HP913—Exposing Amber

Don't miss out on any of our super romances. Write to us at the following address for information on our newest releases and club information.

Heartsong Presents Readers' Service
PO Box 721
Uhrichsville, OH 44683

Or visit www.heartsongpresents.com

Praying for
Rayne

Elizabeth Goddard

Heartsong Presents

Thank you to Roger Weinlaeder of the Weinlaeder Seed Company for sharing his expertise in North Dakota farming, and to Deborah Vogts, dear friend and critique partner, for her assistance in making the farm scenes resonate. A very special thanks to another dear friend, Shannon McNear, for her commitment and dedication in helping me to polish and edit my manuscripts and for helping me take the stories deeper. Thanks to friends and writing buddies Lynette Sowell and Lisa Harris for being there with me from the beginning, and to Ellen Tarver for her exceptionally keen eyes.

A note from the Author:
I love to hear from my readers! You may correspond with me by writing:

Elizabeth Goddard
Author Relations
PO Box 721
Uhrichsville, OH 44683

ISBN 978-1-61626-114-6

PRAYING FOR RAYNE

Scripture taken from the New American Standard Bible, © 1960, 1962, 1963, 1968, 1971, 1972, 1973, 1975, 1977, 1995 by The Lockman Foundation. Used by permission

Our mission is to publish and distribute inspirational products offering exceptional value and biblical encouragement to the masses.

PRINTED IN THE U.S.A.

one

Symmetrical curves and spiraling waves rained over the cornfields and danced across the page. . . .

"Rayne Carolyn Flemming." Hands on hips, Rayne's mother stood in the doorway, matching perfectly the antique fixtures in the old farmhouse. "Just what do you think you're doing?"

Rayne allowed her a slim smile, thinking that her mother appeared much older than her age. At forty-five, she'd never dream of putting color on her hair to hide the gray or dressing in anything that she hadn't kept in her closet for fifteen years. Even when her clothes had been nice and new, they had still looked frumpy.

Hating her negative thoughts, Rayne tugged another drawing from where it was pinned to the yellow and blue floral wallpaper—a design from years gone by. She sighed. "You make it sound like I'm ten, Mom."

Her mother strode all the way into her daughter's bedroom and placed a hand on the drawings Rayne held then tugged gently. "Let me have those."

Rayne held on. "I need them."

Her mother gave up in exasperation. "What on earth for?"

"I can use these at work." Rayne thumbed through the various sketches she'd pinned to her bedroom wall over the years. Noticing one of her favorites, she slipped it from the stack to peruse more closely. Spirals and waves stared back at her— maybe nothing special to anyone else, but Rayne saw beauty in the patterns. She saw water designs she could use in her job at FountainTech.

Standing next to her, her mother appeared to study the sketch as well. "I know I don't understand what your pictures mean, but they remind me of you. I want to keep your drawings on the wall."

Her mother made it sound as if Rayne had died and the wall was her memorial. Rayne put the sketches on her bed and opened her briefcase to place them inside. "You don't have to keep this as my room, you know. I'm a big girl now. You might even consider redecorating with something new and fresh, make it into a guest room. Dad could use it for an office."

"Nope, I couldn't do that. Your father would never agree. He hopes. . ."

Rayne heard the trembling in her mother's voice. Would they ever let their only child go? "I know. He hopes I'll come home." She wished she'd received news about the promotion she expected before she'd come home for the Christmas holidays. Her success would go a long way to convince her parents she was serious about her work. And maybe, just maybe, they'd believe in her.

"That, and he hopes you'll reconsider Paul's offer. We're farmers, Rayne. This is the life you know. And your father worries about you all alone in the city."

"Fargo? The city? Get serious, Mom." Ah. Stay a farm girl. Marry the boy next door. Why couldn't she eagerly oblige her parents by fulfilling those simple expectations? Be happy with an otherwise uneventful life, though it was a hard life. Her father worked himself to the marrow, as did her mother. This previous year had been bad for their wheat—too much rain.

Rayne zipped up the soft leather pocket holding her sketches and laptop and tugged the briefcase flap over, effectively closing it. She looked around her room. Two pieces from her Samsonite luggage sat on the floor. Everything was tidy, just as her mother had required of her when she was growing up.

"That should do it." Rayne tugged her briefcase strap over her shoulder and lifted a suitcase with each hand.

"Oh no you don't. Your father can get those if you insist on leaving." Rayne's mother huffed. "I don't see why you have to go just yet. Aunt Margaret will be here this afternoon. I'm sure she made the red velvet cake you like so much. Can't you stay a little longer?"

Rayne descended the staircase, still carrying her luggage, her mother following close behind. Guilt heaped on more guilt. That's what her mother did. "I've been here two weeks already, and I should have driven back yesterday."

"But yesterday was New Year's Eve, and you can't drive on New Year's Day."

By the time Rayne reached the bottom of the stairs, her shoulder had begun to ache along with her nerves. She dropped the luggage and slipped the briefcase from her arm, setting it on the floor. Voices resounded from the kitchen.

". . .if this weather keeps up."

"Yah betcha," her father replied. His voice, bold and strong, was always a comfort to Rayne.

"Oh, that must be Paul." Rayne's mother hurried past and headed to the small country kitchen of the farmhouse.

The familiar voice conversing with her father sent dread through Rayne. Maybe North Dakotan farmers were tenacious by nature, their perseverance having evolved over decades in order to survive. That's why her parents continued to plant seeds in her, hoping for her return. That's why Paul Frasier continued to plant seeds in her, hoping she'd agree to marry him.

She strolled into the kitchen, expecting to hear a discussion about how cold it was outside and what the weather would do over the next several days. In the Flemming home, the conversation never veered much from the weather. The weather could make or break farmers.

Rayne smiled at her father, who was piling bacon high on a platter already filled with eggs. "You know what they say—the cold keeps out the riff-raff."

Paul's eyes brightened when he saw her. "Rayne, I didn't realize you were still here."

What? You didn't see my car parked outside? Rayne smiled, playing along. "Yep, still here for five more minutes."

His smile dimmed. "You're heading back to Fargo to work at the water company?"

Paul knew perfectly well. It wasn't like him to make jabs. "It's called FountainTech, remember?"

"Oh, that's right." Paul removed his jacket then took the cup of coffee her mother offered. The man was tall and handsome, with strong, rugged Norwegian ancestry. He owned and ran a successful farm. Why hadn't she been able to bring herself to say yes when he'd finally proposed?

Her father set the platter on the table as he peered at her through sad, disapproving eyes. He'd never been impressed with her career. She wasn't sure he even understood what she did exactly. Something inside her seemed to crack like the smallest of leaks in a water main—at one time she had held her father's appreciative gaze. She longed to see that again. She longed to please him, but at what cost? Giving up her dream? Suddenly, her throat constricted.

Uncomfortable silence filled the kitchen.

"Paul, care to join us for breakfast?" her mother asked to be polite, though to Rayne's ears it sounded more like an attempt to change the subject and keep the peace.

"No, thank you, Carol. I've already eaten. Just wanted to stop by to see how you were doing."

"All right then." Her mother busied herself making toast.

Paul and her father took seats at the small table and started up their conversation again while her father ate. It seemed they had nothing else to say to the traitor. When she'd graduated with an art degree, they hadn't considered it a real education. Why would she expect them to consider her work as a water feature designer to be a real job? Part of her wished she didn't care what her family members thought of her chosen career because she loved it so much. Why couldn't they love it, too, instead of withholding their approval?

She loved designing fountains, choreographing the water

into art that was emotionally dramatic. Right now she couldn't wait to get back to her job.

Rayne drew in a breath to soften the tension in her neck and breathed in the aroma of breakfast, mingled with the mustiness of a farmhouse built in 1900.

"I need to head back to Fargo, so I'll say my good-byes now," she said, interrupting their conversation.

Holding a plate of toast, her mother froze midstride as though surprised to hear the news. She set the plate on the table and wiped her hands against her apron, a resigned look on her face. "We'll help you out, Rayne. Won't we, Gary?"

Rayne's father nodded. "I'll get your bags."

Finally, Rayne stood next to her car—a white Volkswagen Passat she'd bought when she landed her job—and hugged her mother and father. Paul wished her well. She looked at the small house behind them, laced with the remnants of yesterday's snow. She committed to memory today's characteristics of the house where she grew up. She'd felt loved, safe, and secure. That's what had made these last few years so difficult.

Once her parents knew of her promotion and saw her success, they'd know she had made the right decision. But doubt—maybe all the seeds planted into the soil of her heart over the last two weeks—had wreaked havoc on her confidence.

Have I made the right decision?

Though she'd sought an answer from God, He'd been silent on the matter.

&

Jack Kostner pressed his chest to his leg, feeling the stretch in his hamstring. Wouldn't do to injure himself on his first day of work.

Alone on the racquetball court, he stretched tall. Drawing in a breath, he noted the air was devoid of that stale sock and locker room odor—something he could expect to experience once the health club filled with bodies again.

But not at 5:00 a.m.

Jack began slamming the ball—he didn't need a partner to get his practice in. Considering he was new to Fargo and the health club, he'd cut himself some slack. A partner would turn up soon enough, though sometimes he wasn't sure if he wanted one.

Someone pounded on the Plexiglas wall behind him. Breathing hard, Jack caught the ball and glanced at the lanky man dressed in workout shorts and looking eager. Jack could guess at his reason for disturbing him.

The man opened the door and leaned in. "You expecting someone? Or could you use a challenge?"

Jack laughed. Nobody ever beat him. This guy was in for it. "Sure. But I've only got forty-five minutes to play." After that he'd shower and head to work—the first day on his new job. He'd spent last night setting up his office so he could get down to business today. No slacking for him.

The man raised his eyebrows. "More like fifteen for me."

"That'll do." Without another word, Jack slammed a fast serve, catching the man off guard.

They soon fell into the rhythm of the game, the ball bouncing around the walls. Jack loved the sound of it and the smell of the rubbery sphere as it darted around the cube encasing them.

After half an hour, Jack paused and pressed his hands against his thighs, breathing hard. The guy had beaten him three games already.

"I thought you said you only had fifteen minutes," Jack managed.

His opponent's eyes widened. "Yep. I'd better run." He rushed to the door then turned back to Jack. "Name's Carl."

Still gasping for breath, Jack nodded. "Jack."

Carl smiled and exited the court. Jack knew he'd see the man again. He'd have another chance to play and beat him next time. Chagrined, he headed for the shower.

He wondered at his sour start to the day. Usually nobody

beat Jack Kostner. At racquetball or otherwise. Still, playing with someone better was a sharpening of the iron, as the saying went. Even though he hated losing, he enjoyed being challenged and, yes, being honed. He wondered if he would find anyone at FountainTech to challenge him, sharpen his ideas and creations. If it would make him better, he'd welcome the competition.

Once an Imagineer—imagination engineer—at Disney, Jack had no plans to be bested. Only a fool ever quit growing and learning. Jack shoved through the door to the showers. Yep. The only thing he'd ever been a quitter at was love. But that wasn't his fault. His fiancé had skipped out on him two days before their wedding last year.

Two days!

And that's why he found himself in North Dakota, being beaten at racquetball at five in the morning.

After his stint in the special effects department at Disney, his experience and education in engineering and product design had come in handy at Elemental Innovations, Inc., that is, until he'd met and fallen in love with Kiera Stemmons.

And she was still working at Elemental in sunny California while he was shivering in the cold up north. She'd almost destroyed him. He'd had nothing left. Jack showered and dressed, furious with himself for letting his mind go there. Fargo was a new start for him, empty of all reminders of that woman.

But hadn't God seen his pain?

Stop!

Fuming, he tugged on his socks. *Get a grip, man.*

Okay, Jack was back. At twenty-seven he'd learned his lessons and was ready to throw all of his energy into this company's water fountain designs.

Once he stepped through the exit doors of the health club and onto the snow-lined pavement, the cold slammed him. He wondered if working out this early and then hitting the frigid air was good for a person—could it constrict his blood vessels and give him a heart attack like his grandfather?

With that thought, his mind drifted to his parents and their tragic death. He stiffened and shoveled the thoughts away like so much snow.

Heading to his car, Jack prodded himself to focus on FountainTech, get on with his new life. Why wouldn't the brooding thoughts leave him alone? Maybe it was the lack of sunshine. He was accustomed to jogging outside in the sunshine every morning. Couldn't the cloudy darkness of winter give a person some sort of depression?

Enough. He wouldn't let buried memories of Kiera or his parents bring him down. Jack started his jet black Pontiac Solstice and, despite the snow and sludge, spun from the parking lot.

two

"Hold that door!" Rayne called, catching Heidi's eyes.

Heidi held the elevator door for her with a smile, while others appeared annoyed. Rayne gasped for breath when she stepped into the elevator. She hated being late. Her workday started at eight, and it was five till now. Rayne liked to be at work an hour early to organize her thoughts.

Surrounded by a few of her coworkers, as well as others she didn't know, Rayne felt like a sardine in the elevator.

"How were your holidays, Rayne?" Heidi asked.

Rayne felt drab and mousy next to Heidi, who had green eyes and beautiful, long blond hair. *Gorgeous.* She made Rayne conscious of her dull brown, shoulder-length cut. Maybe she was like her mother after all; she had never considered doing anything to her hair to make it vibrant.

"Good, but I was ready to be home," she replied. The word *home* sounded strange on her tongue when using it to describe her apartment in Fargo.

Kathy, a tall, lanky girl from accounting, laughed as though she understood, also having left Fargo to see family. Did everyone go through the frustration of failing their families, as Rayne did? Or did others live up to the expectations placed on them?

"My parents came to see me." Heidi rubbed her nose. "Can't have Christmas without the grandkids."

For a moment, an image of holding a baby flashed in Rayne's mind. If she'd said yes to Paul and married him months ago, might she be pregnant by now? Of course, as a farmer's wife, a brood of children was expected, and right away. She chuckled inside but sobered as she was reminded once again of why her parents wanted her to marry Paul. As

13

an only child, she was their only hope for grandchildren. A marriage to Paul would guarantee the grandbabies stayed close. Just another reason for her parents to hold on to her so tightly.

The elevator doors finally swooshed open, and the FountainTech employees poured out into a small entrance hall. To the left were glass doors, the main entrance to FountainTech. A door on the right of the hall allowed employees through the back entrance, a quicker path to their offices on that side. Kathy headed right, punching the entry code into the keypad to open the back door.

Rayne, Heidi, and two others strolled through the reception area, still wearing their coats, hats, and gloves. Rayne began shedding her winter gear.

Gail, FountainTech's perky receptionist, smiled as they went past. "Coffee's already made."

"That sounds wonderful. I'm chilled to the bone." Rayne exited the reception area into the main hallway. Her office was two doors down on the right. She opened the door, flipped on the light, and took in a deep breath.

Ah, she loved the smell of her office. And by this afternoon, maybe she could even say that success never smelled so sweet, because by then she might have heard about her promotion. She left the door open to hear the telltale sounds of employees as they arrived. She loved being back at work.

Giddy with excitement for what today—what this week— could bring, Rayne was overwhelmed. Humbled. She never stopped being amazed at the sort of talent walking the halls of FountainTech.

Astounding talent. In comparison, Rayne might consider herself ordinary—if not for her designs. She was on the creative team at FountainTech and had demonstrated a unique ability to pull the team together, guiding its direction. She'd also created the company's latest design, now in production. The vice president, Harold Cullins, had spoken to her about her talent and asked if she was interested in managing the team. She knew the position was open, and he'd assured her she would have it.

But that was weeks ago.

After setting the folder with her old drawings on her desk, she hung her coat and stuffed her gloves and hat in the pockets. A glance out her window gave her a good view of Fargo and a few distant fields, snow clinging to both the city and landscape.

A light knock on her door drew her attention. She hadn't taken a seat yet. She looked up to see Barb standing in the doorway holding out an extra cup of coffee.

"Is that for me?"

Barb smiled. "Of course. I couldn't wait for you to get here. You're running late today."

Rayne savored the warm cup as she wrapped her hands around it. She slurped the hot yumminess before answering. "Had too much snow to shovel off my car this morning. Maybe I can move into an apartment with a garage soon." Yep, right after she heard about her promotion.

Barb's eyes twinkled as if she had a secret.

"What?"

The tall brunette laughed. "Have you seen him?"

Rayne shook her head and took a sip of coffee then pulled out her chair. "Seen who?"

She began pulling her sketches from the folder and spreading them across her desk. Time to get the creative juices flowing. They had a new design contract to fulfill.

"The new guy, who else?" Barb asked.

The designs on Rayne's desk were quickly stealing her attention from Barb. Though crude and rough, the drawings still had merit; even the ones she'd drawn ten years ago had a glimmer of creativity in them.

Barb tugged on her arm. "Come on. You've got to see him."

Rayne stared up at her friend. "You've got to be kidding, right? We're not in high school here."

"Yeah, well, professionals or not, this guy is gorgeous. I

don't want you to be shocked and have your mouth hang open the first time you see him like Margie did."

Rayne almost lost her coffee at the comment. "I don't think you have to worry about me doing that."

She was interested in one thing—getting her promotion. Besides, handsome men didn't do a thing for her. If the time came when she thought she was ready to settle down, become a wife and mother, she knew that a good husband could be found only in a man who had a good heart.

Barb looked wounded. "Are you kidding? You don't want to see?"

Rayne shook her head. "I'm sure I'll meet him soon enough. I've got to get my thoughts into my work now."

Her fellow employee stepped into the doorway and peered down the hallway. She looked back at Rayne and frowned. Rayne heard someone she couldn't see whisper to Barb.

Barb glanced back at Rayne. "He's in his office now anyway. Door's closed. Sorry I bothered you."

Rayne felt badly. Barb was a member of the creative team, and Rayne would soon be her boss. "How about lunch?"

Barb's expression softened, and she shrugged. "Lunch sounds good."

Voices continued to resound in the hall as the eighty or so employees of FountainTech entered the workplace. To Rayne's chagrin, she heard more whispers about the new guy—his abilities and talents and good looks. It didn't sound as if anyone knew what he'd been hired to do, but the FountainTech employee roster had grown along with the company's glowing reviews and client list. A new employee wasn't unusual.

Rayne shut her door, silencing the gossip.

≈

With the door to his office closed, Jack perused the files of the creative design team he would be managing.

Of course, the vice president of the company, Harold Cullins, had used the exceptional talent at the company to convince Jack to accept his offer. He wasn't sure he'd believed Harold's claims, but it was a great opportunity to come aboard a growing company near its inception. Never mind that he'd wanted to escape California.

He swiped a hand down his face and stood to stare out his window. It had started snowing again. A little bit of snow in San Diego would shut the place down.

Turning back to his desk, he fingered the files of those people he considered the most gifted—the top three members of his team.

One of them stood out above the rest. He flipped through the hard copy of some of her designs. Impressive.

Sitting again, he studied the 3-D design models of her drawings on his laptop. She might very well be the iron to sharpen iron, the challenge he—

The door flew open, Harold occupying the space. "There you are, champ."

Startled by the intrusion, Jack minimized his screen. Hadn't the man ever heard of knocking? Jack didn't like being called "champ" either. His first day was getting off to a great start already.

Harold was at least six-two and appeared to enjoy that he intimidated people. In his fifties, his hair was completely gray, a statement of experience to back up his imperious attitude. His gaze did a 180 around Jack's office, noting the awards and photographs Jack had put up last night.

Jack liked that Harold appeared momentarily taken aback. Jack slipped his hand over his mouth to hide his smile and leaned back in his chair to watch the vice president.

Harold came fully into the office, closing the door behind him. "You've been busy, I see." He took the seat across from Jack's desk and propped his ankle across his knee.

"I came in last night to get organized. No point in wasting time on that during the day."

"That's what I like about you, Jack. You don't waste any time."

Jack wondered if this conversation would be a waste of time. But he couldn't exactly ask that.

"I came in here to inform you we're meeting at nine."

His thoughts scrambling, Jack nodded.

"I plan to introduce you to the company and specifically to your team. Are you ready?"

"Always."

"Another good trait and one of the reasons I hired you. Plan to keep a low profile until then."

Without another word, Harold rose and left Jack to think.

Did Harold want a PowerPoint presentation for the meeting? Jack wondered if he had been right to think that someone on the creative design team would be his challenger. Maybe Harold would be the one to keep him on his toes.

Jack twisted from his chair and out the door. Harold may not have wanted the news of Jack's position to get out until the meeting, but he needed some caffeine. Surely he could manage to grab some coffee without blowing his cover.

He trotted down the burgundy carpeted hall and past the tall mahogany doors of the offices, making his way to the kitchen. He'd made sure to take a private tour of the place last night.

The company effectively shut down for two weeks over the holidays, giving all its employees that time in addition to vacation. Unfortunately, the impact of such generosity was apparent as employees lingered in the hallway, chatting it up with each other. "Catching up." In Jack's opinion, the company was now two weeks behind on its projects.

A few women huddled together near the doorway of an office and stopped talking as he drew near. Faces flashed with expectant smiles. They were waiting to meet him, of course. But he walked right past and saluted them, amused when he heard their quiet snickers.

Almost to the kitchen, he rounded a corner and. . .*smack*.

A warm female body slammed against him then jerked away and gasped.

Coffee painted the front of her blouse. She stepped further back and stared down, a look of horror on her face. With her hands held out as if still registering what had just happened, her mouth hung open. Jack noted her lipstick smeared over her upper lip. A pretty pinkish color.

"Here, let me help you." Jack hurried into the kitchen. "Let's clean you up." He grabbed some paper towels and started to press them against the front of her shirt then paused, thinking better of it.

He handed the paper towels to her, seeing her blush. "Thank you," she said, softly.

Kind brown eyes flashed up at him then down his neck where they lingered. "Oh. . .I'm afraid you have lipstick on your collar."

Jack quickly lost his smile. "Lipstick?" Another glance at her lips and he knew.

That was one thing he'd failed to do yet. He liked to keep an extra starched white shirt in his office, just in case there was a coffee mishap. He'd seen it happen a gazillion times.

"If you try to rub off the lipstick, you'll only make it worse, I'm afraid. I'd like to pay to have that cleaned for you."

"And I should pay for getting the coffee out of that blouse. How about we call it even?"

Though Jack wouldn't say she was a beauty—in fact, she was unremarkable—there was something behind her eyes that whispered to him. *This one is a deep thinker.*

She smiled with a disappointed shrug. "I have an important meeting in an hour. I can't stand up in front of everyone like this."

"You should keep an extra blouse in your office for this sort of thing." Jack hung his hands in his pocket, wondering about her role in Harold's announcement. "I'm Jack Kostner, by the way." He thrust his hand out.

She met it with hers, her hand soft and warm. "Rayne Flemming."

I know exactly who you are. Though he'd not seen her

picture, he'd read her file. He'd been right—she was a deep thinker, a creative designer. As far as he could tell, she was the most valuable person on his team.

Jack rocked back and forth on his feet, growing anxious. Normally he'd consider this sort of interaction a waste of time. What was the matter with him?

"You must be the new guy."

"Yep." Jack grinned, but he couldn't say more, Harold's words still fresh in his mind. He focused on getting his coffee, and when he turned around, she was gone.

Jack tugged on his collar. He needed to at least inspect the damage in a mirror. Maybe he could draw his suit jacket tight and look like a nerd but hide the lipstick.

And if not? Harold would introduce Jack, the new employee and manager, and he would stand in front of everyone with lipstick on his shirt.

That would give the women something to talk about.

three

Barb was right. Jack was a looker, with the sort of thick black hair that made a girl want to run her fingers through it, and striking blue eyes that seemed to read her thoughts. He had that strong, rugged jaw and athletic physique she often saw on the cover of magazines while standing in line at the grocery store.

But Rayne wasn't attracted to a man simply for his looks. As for his personality, though, Jack seemed pleasant enough. Warm and friendly.

Rayne glanced at the clock on the wall. Only ten more minutes until the meeting. She fidgeted with her notes—an acceptance speech with details about preparing the team for its next project—doubt creeping in. Before the holidays, Harold had spoken to her in confidence about managing the team, and she'd accepted his offer, though not in writing. In fact, nothing had been in writing, or even set in stone, now that she recalled their exact conversation.

Rayne stood and took a deep breath. Maybe she worried for nothing. Still, why hadn't he spoken to her more specifically about the position? All she could think was that Harold wasn't the sort of manager who coddled. He liked forward thinkers and people who took initiative, who were willing to take what he offered and do something with it.

Unfortunately, that left Rayne unclear about where she stood. She had no way of knowing if his announcement today was regarding her as the new team manager. But she knew the creative team needed a leader, especially on its newest project. If not today, then soon.

Opening her door, she stepped into the hall, joining other employees headed to the small conference room. Of course, only those whose departments were affected would be there to hear Harold's announcement.

Barb appeared, walking beside her. She glanced at Rayne's blouse but said nothing. Rayne figured Barb didn't want to embarrass Rayne further by talking about it in front of everyone.

"So what do you think Harold's going to say?" Barb asked.

Rayne wanted to be excited and expectant, but for the first time since speaking to Harold on the matter of her managing the team, she pushed down her hopes. "I really have no clue."

Questions lingered behind Barb's eyes. "I wonder why he's so hush-hush about it."

Rayne didn't respond, because they'd reached the glass doors of the conference room, held open by one of their fellow employees, Simon Jeffers. He smiled. "Hi there, Rayne."

She replied in kind and thanked him for keeping the door for her. Most of the sixteen chairs around the conference table were occupied except for one seat near the front. The rest of the planning division employees, which accounted for half the company, leaned against the walls, and a few limber ones sat on the floor, legs crossed.

Had that seat been saved for her? Preparing to be formally recognized, if that's what Harold had in mind, Rayne took the only seat left. She set her file in front of her on the table, a little miffed she didn't know what was going on. If Harold announced her today, and she hoped he would, he should have given her fair warning. Then again, to his way of thinking, she knew from experience, he probably thought he had.

She wanted to sigh but stifled it, putting on a confident smile. As she glanced around the room, listening to conversations about the holidays and seeing most of her team there, her confidence ignited once again.

Yep. Harold would announce that he'd promoted her to team manager. She'd been one of the first hired on at FountainTech a year ago at the company's inception, selling herself on her designs alone. She had proven her abilities to coordinate the team's efforts on projects thereafter.

Rayne slowly released a breath and relaxed into the burgundy leather chair. Two people standing against the wall behind her whispered about Jack and his good looks. Rayne fought the desire to look at the ceiling. The culture these days was focused on one thing, it seemed. Rayne couldn't afford for her thoughts to go there, because she wasn't one of the beautiful ones. It would be too depressing. Instead, she considered it a blessing that God had given her more important gifts.

The knob on the door at the head of the conference room clicked, and a hush spread through the room. Harold was obviously standing behind the door, intending to walk through, but held back for some reason. Then the door flew open quickly. *Definitely Harold.*

Tall and authoritative, he stepped through, followed by Jack. A few quiet intakes of breath resounded around the room as though everyone held their breath. Rayne's eye flicked to Jack's collar. The lipstick was barely noticeable—how had he gotten it out? With the way he'd suggested she keep an extra shirt in her office, she supposed he'd dealt with similar situations before. Still, the guy exuded efficiency. Probably kept one of those Tide instant spot removers on hand as well.

She figured the stain could only be seen if one knew where to look. As Harold began to talk, she became self-conscious about her own coffee-stained blouse and leaned against the table, positioning her hands to hide the stain. How was she going to hide that when she stood to make her speech? Expectant and filled with enthusiasm, Rayne snapped her attention back to Harold.

But Harold's announcement had nothing to do with her. Rayne's heart pounded in her throat. She feared the pulse in her neck was like a neon sign to everyone in the room. Harold was introducing Jack. That was odd. There was never fanfare over a regular employee.

Only managers.

Harold peered around the room. Always in command of his audience, he apparently liked to make eye contact with everyone if he could.

"Welcome back from the holidays. I hope you're rested and ready to focus your time and energies on creating the best fountain designs in the world." His deep baritone filled the room like surround sound.

Most cheered their agreement. Harold expected no less. The atmosphere seemed to bubble with anticipation.

"I expect you're wondering why I called this meeting. We needed to get this year started on the right foot. I've hired Jack to manage the design team." It appeared to Rayne that Harold's gaze fell everywhere except on her.

Rayne's heart seemed to stop. She smiled and nodded as if she were excited, fitting in with her fellow employees. When her heart began to beat again, long and loud in her ears, it covered all other sounds. She was in a tunnel, and time seemed to slow around her.

Thump, thump.

Harold's lips were moving, but she heard only the. . .

Thump, thump.

In slow motion, she swiveled her head, scanning the faces around the conference room.

Thump, thump.

Her gaze fell on Barb, smiling against the wall in the back of the room, her full attention on Harold.

Thump, thump.

Then Rayne's head rotated. She was looking at the front of the room. At Jack.

Thump, thump. . .thump, thump. . .

He was staring back at her. Rayne had a terrible thought. Did he know?

❧

Jack loved moments like these. He soared like an eagle, hearing himself announced as the new manager of the design team. He heard Harold speaking, knew the man was introducing him, but his thoughts had already moved on to what he would say when his turn came.

The only glitch in the moment, in his thoughts, was the look on Rayne Flemming's face when Harold made his announcement. Though smiling, the light in her eyes dimmed. She looked as if. . .well, as if the breath had been knocked out of her. Literally.

"You're up, champ."

"Thanks, Harold." Jack smiled and tried not to grit his teeth at the nickname Harold had branded him with. A splinter in his hand would have been less annoying.

Pouring all his energy into appearing enthusiastic, Jack stepped to the front, and Harold eased back against the wall.

Definitely, Jack was back. Today was the premier of his show. He didn't slow to acknowledge the prick of fear curdling his stomach. Failure wasn't in his plans. Not this time.

"I can't tell you how thrilled I am to be FountainTech's newest member. Even more so because of the talent I'm joining here." He paused, for effect, his momentary silence building expectation in the room.

He clicked his remote wand, and the PowerPoint presentation he'd whipped together within the last hour flashed on to the whiteboard at the front of the room. "Much of this information you already know, but I want to show it to you in a new light, if you will. FountainTech's goal is to be the leading provider of water feature designs around the world."

Jack clicked through the three fountains they'd created in the last year. Two in the United States, one in Egypt. Images of multiple fountains lifting water high into the air, like Old Faithful in Yellowstone National Park, played across the screen in a slide show. Music accompanied each of the images.

"Mm." Jack shook his head and glanced back at his hypnotized group. "No matter how many times I watch that, I'll never stop loving it. It will never cease to mesmerize me or to inspire me.

"These images are part of what drew me to your company. You're probably wondering about my background. I came from a similar design company, Elemental Innovations."

He heard a few whispers in the room. He didn't mention he hadn't worked for EI in over six months. In his opinion, FountainTech was far ahead of his old company, and he was jazzed about this opportunity. "And before that I worked at Disney as an imagination engineer—an Imagineer." He grinned, always loving that title.

"And that's what I want from my team. Anything we can imagine, we can create."

Rayne Flemming unexpectedly came into his mind, and he looked her way, but she had her head down, writing on a notepad. Next, Jack chose a slide with employee names. "If your name is up there, you are a member of the team I'll be managing. Over this next week, I plan to find out your strengths and weaknesses and effectively reorganize things. Expect to meet with me one on one."

Finished with his short presentation, he raised the lighting, noting the hopeful looks and shimmering eyes. Good. Just what he liked to see. "Questions?"

Immediately a hand shot up. A blond at the back of the room. "My name is Heidi. What exactly did you do at the companies where you worked before?"

Oh come on. He'd hoped for something, well, more imaginative. For the next twenty minutes, he answered questions. For some reason, he couldn't get his mind off Rayne. He stood at the end of the table, his pant legs touching the edge. She was seated next to where he stood, looking dazed. Disappointment tried to kill his moment, but it would never beat Jack.

He'd expected much more from Rayne than he'd gotten in her reaction.

When the questions finally ended, Harold moved forward to stand next to Jack.

"Thank you, Jack. I'm sure everyone is as equally impressed

as I am, and eager to get to work."

Too soon the meeting was over. Frankly, Jack loved the attention. But Harold was right. Time to get to work. The employees filed from the room, Rayne in their midst. Jack frowned. He'd intended to speak to her before she left, but she'd simply melted out of the room with the others.

"I knew I was right to hire you, Jack. I know you won't let me down." Harold winked then started to leave as well.

"Harold, can I ask you something?"

The man paused, waiting.

"It's about Rayne Fleming."

Harold's eyes brightened. "She'll be the star of your team. Treat her right."

Jack shook his head. "Something's wrong."

Angling his head, Harold studied Jack. "You read people well, Jack. Several weeks ago, I talked to Rayne about managing the team. She would do a good job, no doubt. But I needed someone less creative and craftier for the job." Harold squeezed Jack's shoulder. "You're the man. Good thing for me you came onto the scene when you did."

Harold grinned, making a clucking sound out of the side of his mouth, then left the conference room.

Jack stared after him. Had he meant crafty in a good way? Or crafty as in scheming and conniving? Jack considered himself highly creative, as well. He stared at the floor, calming his anger.

Rayne's reaction made perfect sense now. Harold had dangled the carrot in her face then offered it to Jack. She'd had no warning. She'd been blindsided. As he gathered up his notes and the flash drive holding his PowerPoint, Jack became worried. Very worried.

The most valuable person on his team, Rayne Flemming, could very well leave the company over this. Jack rushed out of the conference room, only one thought pressing him.

I can't afford to lose her. . . .

four

"The higher your aim, the harder your fall." Her father's words—spoken in a rare moment when he'd revealed his own life's disappointments—seemed to mock her.

Tears seared the back of Rayne's eyes, where she kept them imprisoned. She needed time to order her thoughts. Lunch couldn't come fast enough, but now she wished she hadn't invited Barb to join her. At the time, she'd wanted to appease Barb, and she admitted to herself, she'd been counting on having something to celebrate. Maybe she could use her coffee-stained shirt as an excuse—she needed to change into a new one.

With the back of her hand, Rayne brushed away the lone tear that had managed to slip past her guard. Tears had no place in the corporate world.

She leaned against the windowsill. From the fifth floor, she could see a good bit of Fargo, though the view was somewhat obstructed by a few other tall buildings that stood near the bank where FountainTech leased offices. Snow clung to the rooftops and edged the streets and sidewalks, and though the white stuff was as familiar to her as her mother's voice, today it chilled her soul.

How had she so grossly misunderstood Harold's intentions toward her career? Or had the fault been his—dangling the promotion, knowing from the beginning how important this goal was to her. Was it simply an oversight, or was it intentional? Regardless, she'd assigned far too much significance to the promotion, thinking of it as a fleece that would let her know that she'd made the right decision when she'd left home and left her parents' expectations unfulfilled.

Would she be like Gideon and continue to question God?

She scoffed out loud. It was ridiculous to have considered Harold's decision a fleece to begin with. Promotion or no promotion, she could no more give up this dream of creating her designs than air or water. She admitted to herself that, although she'd not been indifferent to the prospect of the boost to her career, this promotion had been all about proving herself to her parents. Her current position wasn't enough to earn their approval.

The big question now was, where would she go from here? How should she react? She'd better figure that out and quickly. The questions assailed her like a blizzard in her mind, lashing at all her neatly constructed plans, ideas about who she was and where she wanted to go, blinding her to the future.

In the distance, the sky began to clear, and the snow clouds, having spent their load, were beginning to push out. Focusing on the blue edging the horizon, Rayne drew in a weighty breath.

A whiff of burnt popcorn seeped under her door. She hated that her office was so close to the kitchen—something else she'd thought would change after this morning's meeting. Tugging her chair back from the desk, she sank into it, longing for her earlier enthusiasm. She had a new boss now. Someone else to impress.

A light knock startled her. "Come in."

The door slowly opened, and there stood Jack. Panic whirled inside. She wasn't prepared to face him yet but forced a smile. "Hi there."

He slipped in and gently shut the door behind him. "Can we talk?"

"Of course."

He was handling her with kid gloves. He knew. . . .

Sitting in the chair on the other side of her desk, he raised his face and studied the sketches on her walls while she studied him. His clean-shaven, strong jaw and the sparkle in his blue eyes bore the enthusiasm she lacked. But she wouldn't let him see that.

She examined his collar. "How did you do that?"

He shook his head as if her question had given him a start. "I'm sorry?"

Despite her mood, she laughed easily. Jack Kostner had a way about him. "My lipstick. . .er. . .the lipstick on your collar. It's all but gone." She put a hand to her face, feeling the heat.

Instantly, a grin brought dimples into his cheeks. "I got lucky. I found a bottle of Wite-Out in the back of a drawer."

Rayne pursed her lips into a smile and quirked a brow. "That *is* lucky."

Jack turned his attention back to her drawings and stood, taking a step toward the wall. Looking closely at one of her sketches, he tilted his head. "How long have you been drawing these?"

Was this some sort of trick question? "Oh, those are from years ago. I know they're nothing brilliant. I just like to be reminded, to be inspired."

He jerked his head to her, his gaze intense. "Oh, you're wrong. They *are* brilliant. In our business, this sort of creativity means everything."

Sitting again, he tugged the chair forward so he could lean on her desk. He was much closer now. Too close for comfort. Oddly, his nearness made her heart race.

"Thank you," she said. "What did you want to see me about?"

Jack eased back now, his fingers over his lips in a thoughtful pose. Her impression of him during his presentation was that he was an aggressive overachiever. By the end of his dynamic and motivating speech, she realized why she hadn't gotten the job. As hard as she tried, that just wasn't her. But now she was seeing a different side to him. A thoughtful side—at least it appeared that way.

"You should already know from my presentation that I planned to meet with each member of the design team individually."

Rayne swallowed and nodded. *Pick up your game, girl. The pacing is faster now.* "Yes, and you planned to reorganize the team based on the members' strengths. What have you decided about me?"

Jack grinned again. She felt a tickle in her stomach—unwelcome and unexpected.

"You're right to the point. I like that. I haven't begun to reorganize yet. I'm simply here, Rayne, to tell you that I had no idea, and that I'm sorry."

Now it was her turn to be startled. She shook her head. "What are you talking about?"

"I know you were expecting the position I now hold. It would have been a promotion for you."

Uneasiness hung in the air of her office. She struggled to think what to say. His apology was completely unexpected. And unusual.

"What you need to know is that you're vital to this company, to this team, and to my vision to make FountainTech the leader in water feature designs."

Jack was pouring it on thick. Rayne's heart pounded in her ears again. The room grew stuffy.

Just breathe.

Is this how they extracted performance from their people at Disney? Whatever magic Jack was using, it was working.

Her enthusiasm stirred once again, but she cautioned herself. Was he friend or foe? What reason did she have to trust the man she'd lost her promotion to? And the fact remained she'd lost her chance to gain the praise she wanted from her family. She clung to the uncertainty of her renewed enthusiasm and her wariness as though it were her only lifeline.

"So, Rayne, what do you like to be reminded of?"

Rayne stared.

"You said earlier about your sketches, you put them up because you like to be reminded of. . .something. What was it?"

He dropped his smile, and at once his gaze turned intense.

Again. Rayne would need about a gallon of coffee every morning to keep up with him. Still, his energy made her feel alive. She considered his question. Did she want to share so much of herself just yet?

Regretting that she'd made the comment, Rayne focused on tracing a knot in the veneer of the maple desk. Jack leaned forward again. Too close.

"The inspiration for those designs came from the wheat, soybean, corn, and sunflower fields on my parents' farm. When the wind blows, waves ripple across the fields. As a child, that fascinated me. I spent hours drawing what I saw. Then when my dad tried various irrigation systems, I was even more intrigued with the synchronization of the water streams and what happened when the wind disrupted them."

Jack stared at her for what seemed like an eternity. "If there is magic on this planet, it is contained in water," he said, in an almost-whisper.

Rayne laughed softly. "Who said that?"

"I forget exactly. Some scientist at the University of Pennsylvania." Jack wore that thoughtful expression again, as if he had gone to a place so far away that Rayne could never join him there.

૱

The air in Jack's office grew stale. He opened the door, inviting in what he hoped was fresh air from the hallway. It was already six, and most everyone was gone for the day, so he wasn't worried about any unwelcome intrusions. His first day had gone by far too fast, filled with meetings and unintentional conversations not of his making. But, he supposed, it was part of the process of settling into his new position.

Harold had popped in on several occasions, swinging the door open without knocking. That was quickly becoming the man's MO. Jack would have to be much more deliberate in his effort to get work done in the face of interruptions. He'd obviously taken time for granted, believing he had plenty available to accomplish his tasks and achieve his goals.

Add to that a special project that filled his evenings, and he certainly couldn't afford to waste his daytime hours.

Pulling together the stack of files on his desk, he hated that he'd only made it through half of them. A water fountain feature danced elegantly across his computer screen. Fluid and comforting, his thoughts went right to the creator. *Rayne.*

She'd turned him down for lunch, saying she had to change into a clean shirt. A valid excuse. He'd have done the same in her shoes. He was fairly sure she wouldn't be leaving the company anytime soon—she seemed obsessed with her creations. Still, he'd keep reminding her of her importance to the team. She was his biggest asset in the company. He should keep her close and bolster her if she became discouraged.

Stuffing the files into a desk drawer, he laughed a little at the thought. She'd be near him regardless, because they needed to work together on the new water fountain designs. Tomorrow he'd talk to her about her thoughts on their next design project.

He began the process of shutting down his laptop then stopped it, the design dancing on the screen, compelling him to watch. Rayne had programmed the features into the computer, and in the lab, the engineers and technicians had built and organized the various water-pumping mechanisms and software-driven nozzles that brought the fountain to life. Rubbing his chin, Jack wondered, *Would a working model of this fountain still be set up in the lab?*

Only one way to find out. Whistling, Jack strode out of his office and down the hallway to the elevators. FountainTech's lab—where they tested their designs before installing them for clients—operated in the basement. As he listened to the elevator music, he chuckled. When he'd first heard that FountainTech was located in Fargo, he almost lost his coffee. Texas, or maybe Southern California, but Fargo?

After doing a little more research, he'd learned that quite a few high-tech companies made their home in Fargo. The elevator slowed and stopped. After the door slid open, he stepped onto the basement floor. In a small, empty foyer, double doors stared at him. He punched in his PIN and heard the locking mechanism release.

Jack walked slowly down the dimly lit hallway to the room where the technicians did most of their work. His people created the original designs, but there was much more to building the features. Unfortunately, removing limits from creativity often met with resistance among the technical crowd. But that was part of his job—smoothing things over between the creators and the technicians. Since he was working on his own design—a new water pump for which he would apply for a patent—he could better understand the technical mind's frustration with the creators and planners.

When he neared the lab where he hoped to find the fountain still intact, he heard music playing softly down the hall. He hesitated. Someone else was here.

No matter, he decided, and continued on his way. Possibly he could get some questions answered if one of the technicians had stayed late. Peering through the small window of the door, he saw darkness set off by minimal light. He stepped inside, allowing the door to slip shut quietly behind him; then he crept around computers and a small stadium-like structure to see a stunning water feature—or fountain—choreographed to the theme song of *Out of Africa*. The real thing would work on a much larger scale, of course, but multiple fountains sprang to life from pumps, similar to synchronized swimmers.

Once his eyes adjusted to the dark, he noticed someone standing at the far end of the water theater. Rayne.

Jack's first thought was to walk over to her.

But then. . .he couldn't move. He watched her stare as though she were mesmerized by the fountain's performance. The water danced for her alone.

five

Rayne stood in the darkened room, watching the fountain shoot up in synchronized waves—forward, to the right, then to the left. Nozzles on each side sent sprays darting in between the streams as though weaving fluid—all in perfect time to the music chosen by the client.

As she allowed herself to be drawn into the splendor, the moment, peace surrounded her. She let go of her troubles. If she were given freedom to create such a thing of beauty every day of her life, what did she care if friends and family back home couldn't understand? Her spirits lifted higher and higher until she fancied herself floating on waves of joy.

The fountain she'd designed would be twenty times the size of this one, once installed at the front of the client's financial headquarters. And despite its striking beauty, she doubted that people dashing to and fro would take time to stop and watch the water's performance.

Rayne closed her eyes and turned her face toward an imaginary sun, soaking in the spray that misted her skin. She drew in a deep breath, the scent of water calming her.

Suddenly, she sensed someone next to her. Alarm sent chills up her arms, and her heart jumped into her throat. She opened her eyes.

Jack.

A soft smile on his lips, he was staring at her with that deep, introspective look. What was he thinking?

The momentary peace she'd savored slipped away.

His smile coiled into a frown. "I didn't mean to disturb you."

You didn't? She fought the rising frustration that even here—in her place of peace and joy—the man who'd stolen from her had invaded her world. "No, it's all right." What else could she say to her new boss? It wasn't his fault. He hadn't intentionally stolen the promotion. Giving the position to Jack had been Harold's decision.

In coming here to watch the fountain, Rayne had attempted to silence the questions. Had she allowed this promotion to be taken? Was there something she could have or should have done differently?

"Please." He touched her arm gently, sending a jolt through her, and gestured to the fountain. "Can we watch together?"

No. "Of course."

With Jack standing at her side, Rayne struggled to return to the serenity she'd achieved moments before. Then, slowly, she relaxed. Was there nothing the soothing effect of water couldn't do for her?

In that way, she supposed, the water's comfort reminded her of the Holy Spirit. *"Is there anything too hard for Me?"* the gentle voice seemed to whisper in her heart.

Am I supposed to be here? She waited for an answer to her heart's question.

Silence.

Unsurprised, Rayne sighed and sneaked a glimpse at Jack. His attention was focused on the fountain now rather than her, and with a relaxed expression, he looked much younger. Boyish even. The fountain apparently had the same effect on him. Somehow this reaction they shared gave Rayne a sense that everything would be all right. Maybe the Lord had answered her after all—in His own way.

Or was she simply too self-absorbed, listening to only the answers she wanted to hear, ignoring the voices of those who'd provided for and raised her? God had given her the parents she had, and they considered her a "flighty child," unwilling to settle down to life on the farm.

It wasn't inside Rayne to rebel as much as to simply follow the dream propelled by her gift.

Jack touched her hand, tugging her from her thoughts.

"This is even more impressive than I imagined."

Did he know the part she'd played in its creation? She allowed a smile. "Isn't it?" *And thank you.*

"That is, up close and personal." He stared at her, his eyes brooding.

Was he still referring to the fountain? Jack didn't seem to be the sort of man to get tangled up in sexual harassment.

A knot swelled at the back of her throat. She reminded herself that handsome men did nothing for her. But there was something about Jack. He was. . .like her.

They had a connection, something in common. Rayne shook the thoughts away before they planted seeds. The music, the fountain, and the dim lighting had all worked to bring her emotions to the surface.

"Well, I need to get home." She headed over to the controls to begin switching them off. "The plumbing in this room was quite a feat, as you can imagine."

Jack flipped a switch, flooding the large room with light. Thankfully, the bright lighting changed the unbidden romantic atmosphere.

❧

Jack squinted at the lights and glanced around the large watertight room. Must have cost some bucks. He'd definitely want to explore, but later. Rayne pulled a lever, and the fountain pumps slowly lost momentum, the water spurting until it stopped.

Her shirt was crisp and white, reminding him of their collision earlier in the day. "I see you had an opportunity to change your shirt." He winced and pushed a hand over his idiotic mouth. *Great conversation, man.*

"I told you I planned to go home and change at lunch," she said with a quick glance and partial grin while she focused on shutting off the rest of the fountain.

"According to your file, you were the chief designer of this water feature. It's amazing."

Though her mouth remained neutral, the smile behind her

eyes told him she was pleased at his compliment. "We work as a team around here. I can't take all the credit."

"You're right. But although teamwork is important, there has to be a creative lead. You're it."

When she didn't respond but instead turned her attention to clicking keys on the computer, shutting down the driving software, he chuckled and looked down at the floor, feeling heat in his neck. He wanted to give credit where credit was due, encourage an employee who needed it, but this felt more like. . . *No!*

He was *not* flirting. Jack studied her. Rayne Flemming wasn't a striking beauty. Her nose was too rounded and her cheeks were a little pudgy. Her hair was a drab brown, and she wore it simple and shoulder length, rather than styled in the latest fashion—things he never would have noticed except that he had once been engaged to the queen of fashion.

To Kiera, there was nothing more important than the newest hairstyle or the latest fashion trend. All her energy had been put into her appearance, leaving nothing on the inside. Like an empty box that was beautifully wrapped, once the package was opened you were disappointed. The gift had been a facade. It wasn't real.

Then there was Rayne. She had that farm girl natural look. There was something about her, though, in her eyes that whispered to a place deep inside him, stirring him. Whatever "it" was might as well have been spoken in Ukrainian for all he understood about why it touched him so. But he suspected it had everything to do with what was on the inside of her— something real, something of value.

A treasure beyond price.

Enough!

Before he realized it, Rayne was striding past him. "Are you leaving or staying?"

He stared, lost in thought.

"Do you want me to flip the light off now, or are you staying?"

Right. Ukrainian. Finally, he snapped out of it and understood her question. "I'm leaving, too. Uh, wait. No, I'm staying." He scratched his head.

Rayne laughed softly then left his sight. From where he remained, he heard the door swoosh open, then shut, signaling her departure. He exhaled slowly.

There were at least six more members of the design team whose files he had yet to preview. He had a feeling, though, that none of them were in the same league with Rayne Flemming. And the more he thought about it, the more he worried that he wasn't in her league either. She would definitely be one to challenge and sharpen him.

As he strolled around the room and examined the pumping mechanisms and nozzles, comparing them to the design he'd been developing on his own in the evenings, he couldn't shut down the niggling. Could he stay focused on the task and succeed at making his dreams for FountainTech and his life come true while working with Rayne?

Why did she distract him so?

six

That evening Rayne trudged up the steps of her second-floor apartment. For the weeks before the holidays, after Harold had mentioned a promotion to her, Rayne had driven around different neighborhoods, considering what sort of house she might like to buy, eventually. Although first, she just planned to move into a larger apartment with a garage for her car.

But a house did not a home make, or at least that's what her mother always told her. She unlocked the door to her apartment and kicked it shut behind her, then turned on the lights. Looking around her lonely apartment, she agreed that her mother had a point. Shedding her coat, she tugged her cell from the pocket.

Her mother had called earlier in the day, but Rayne hadn't recovered from the blow of not getting the promotion and wasn't in the right frame of mind to return the call. Though her mood hadn't improved, Rayne nevertheless called her mother, knowing she'd have to explain if she didn't. The phone rang several times. As she waited for her mother to answer, she thought of the tinny sound the old rotary-dial phone made when she would call someone from her parents' phone.

"Hello?" her mother answered.

"Mom, hi. Sorry, I didn't have the chance to call you back earlier." Rayne forced enthusiasm into her voice. Maybe the action would bring her heart around.

"You had a busy day, then. That's all I wanted to know. How was your first day back at work?" Pots and pans clanked in the background. Rayne pictured the phone cord stretching all over the kitchen as her mother worked and talked on the phone.

Closing her eyes, Rayne could imagine herself at home. "What are you making?"

"Pork roast. Mashed potatoes, that corn I canned last summer."

Rayne drew in a breath of stale air and tried to imagine the aroma of a home-cooked meal. "Sounds good."

"You could enjoy this if you were here."

Mom, please don't. Not now. "The first day back at work after a break is always a hard one. I'm tired. I need to go."

"Hold on."

Rayne could detect the faint sound of water boiling as a lid was lifted.

"I've got to pour the water off the potatoes now. Before you go, I wanted to give you some news."

"What's that?" Rayne opened her refrigerator. Was there anything edible inside?

"Turns out that Paul has some business in Fargo this week."

"Hmm." A tub of burnt orange Tupperware stared back at her. Mom had sent fried chicken with Rayne. She'd forgotten.

"He might stop by to see you."

Rayne pursed her lips, relieved her mother couldn't see, though she wasn't sure why it mattered. "Okay, thanks for telling me." Grabbing the chicken and a Coke, she shut the door with her elbow. "I'll call you this weekend."

"I love you."

"I love you, too."

Before she could take a bite of a drumstick, someone knocked on her door. With a look through the peephole, relief swept over her. She imagined Paul standing outside her door. She opened it with a smile. "Hey, Theresa, come in."

Her petite brunette neighbor stepped inside and shut the door, tugging off her red mittens and navy wool coat. "It's cold out there."

"Welcome to North Dakota." Rayne took a bite of her chicken.

Theresa rubbed her hands together. "I wish these apartments had fireplaces."

"You can get one."

"Yeah, for more money." Theresa smiled and sat on the edge of the sofa.

"Well, I do have this." Rayne turned on the television and the DVD player. The cozy image of a fire roaring in a fireplace filled the screen.

Theresa laughed. "Gotta love technology." She turned her attention to Rayne. "So, any news yet?"

Rayne washed down the chicken with her Coke. She shook her head, knowing what Theresa was asking. The girl next door was the only person she'd shared her hopes with.

"They brought in someone outside of the company for that position."

"Oh Rayne. I'm so sorry."

"I think I'm going to live. Want some fried chicken?"

Theresa nodded. "Sounds good."

After offering Theresa the Tupperware filled with chicken, Rayne took another bite of her drumstick, savoring her mother's cooking—something she definitely missed here. Together she and Theresa ate dinner while they watched a game show. But Rayne couldn't push Jack's face from her mind. He'd seemed to touch a chord somewhere inside her.

She didn't dare harbor an emotional connection with her boss. What was the matter with her?

❧

Jack shuffled through Simon's conceptual drawings as the guy explained his ideas about the structure and sculpture of water. It had taken Jack more time than he'd expected to meet with his team members individually, getting to know them like he planned, and he hadn't finished yet. Interruptions, phone calls, and meetings made each workday speed by before he could accomplish his goals.

Now, two weeks later, he was finally concluding one of the last of the private conversations. Understanding each person's gifts, goals, and dreams would go a long way in helping him mold his team together. He'd dug deep into their lives, into their creative sides, and after assessing their strengths and weakness, he tried to fuel their imaginations. But he could feel the effort draining him.

"What do you think?" Simon asked.

"Now all we have to do is put our brilliant heads together on this next project."

"I mean, what do you really think about my ideas?" Simon gave him a pointed stare.

Meeting the look, Jack smiled inside, recognizing some of himself in Simon. "I think these are excellent."

"But where do I fit in to our team as a whole?"

"What are you asking me?" Simon was fishing. Might as well get to the point.

"I want to be creative lead."

"Ah." Jack leaned back, contemplating. "Let me give it some thought."

Simon frowned and sat forward in his seat. "Look, my stuff is better than Rayne's. Just give me a chance."

Jack hated hearing the pain and desperation in Simon's voice. The guy had a lot to learn. Never appear desperate. Maybe someday he'd give him that tip.

"Look, Simon, everyone's gifts are different. One gift is as important as another's." *And some people's gifts are inspiring beyond words.* "That's why I'm here, so I can fit the talents together—like pieces of a puzzle—to create a beautiful picture, or in this case, fountain."

Simon blew out a breath. "Okay. If you say so."

Jack stood to escort Simon to the door, needing a cup of coffee. He squeezed Simon's shoulder. "Your day will come; don't worry." He winked.

Simon nodded, disappointment on his face as he left Jack's office. Rayne stood in the hall and greeted Simon when he passed. Jack wondered how she would react if she knew Simon had just tried to outmaneuver her. The moves were only good when there was talent to back them up.

Rayne leaned against the wall, waiting. "Are you ready? Or should I come back later?"

He hated that his throat grew taut when she was near. "Have a seat while I grab another cup of coffee. Do you want one?"

"No, thank you. I'm good." Entering his office, she strolled past him, leaving a light floral scent in her wake. The room tilted, if only a smidge. She would sink him if he let her.

As he moved down the hall to the kitchen, he considered all the people he'd met with this morning, desperately wishing that someone else could be lead creator, but then again, could he do that to Rayne after already telling her she had the position?

After filling his cup, he headed back to his office. He'd struggled to sleep the last couple of weeks, his mind warning him to steer clear of her. In this morning's meetings, he'd tried hard to inspire the artists he'd met with, pouring his heart and soul into them, but in doing so, he was afraid he left himself open and vulnerable—not a good place to be when Rayne Flemming stepped into his office. At the very least, he should have met with her first, when he was fresh and on top of his game.

That night at the fountain, she'd revived something in him—something he wanted left untouched and undisturbed. And she'd done it on the very first day. In the doorway of his office he paused, shoving a hand through his hair. Fortunately, Barb, whom he'd interviewed earlier in the morning, stood next to Rayne in his office, chatting. Unintentionally, she'd given him a moment to compose himself.

Once Barb spotted him, she smiled brightly and excused herself.

After shutting his door, Jack glided around his desk, set down the mug, and sank into his chair. "Now, where were we?"

"I'm not sure. You've seen my sketches already. Barb said you looked at her designs, asked about her goals for the company."

Jack detected a hint of guarded resistance in Rayne's voice. Probably a good thing, but then, it could impede their creative development. He leaned back, considering her words. "You're right. I have seen your sketches, and you've shared what inspires you. I've already told you that you're creative lead. But you need to understand that others are trying to position themselves."

"Position themselves?"

"When you're the best at something, people are jealous." Even Jack was jealous of her gift. "They want to knock you down, if possible, and take your place." Jack hoped his comments didn't make her think of him taking the position she'd wanted. He needed her to focus on creating the best fountain yet.

Unfortunately, he wasn't sure he could do the same when he was near Rayne.

Rayne's lips parted as she quietly inhaled.

"Simple office politics, Rayne. Don't be surprised at what people will do."

She nodded. "Is there anything else?"

"Yes. Since you're creative lead, you and I will be working closely together. I'll spend more time with you than with the others. At some point, we'll travel to the project site. Do you have a problem with that?" Some part of him hoped she would say she did, in fact, have a problem with it.

Rayne swallowed. "Of course not."

Had she hesitated, or had he imagined it? "Good. Now I need you to dig deep and pull yourself out of this hole."

Eyes wide, her brows knitted. "Excuse me? I don't understand."

"You know what I'm talking about. You wanted this management position. But Harold hired me. You can't lose your creative edge because you didn't make it this time. There will always be other opportunities." Jack winced inside. He was roughing her up a bit. But she needed a good kick. The Rayne he'd collided with on his very first day at work had been enthusiastic and vibrant. That was the day she thought she would be receiving her promotion. He'd not seen that Rayne since he'd become her boss. He knew that the loss of the promotion bothered her. And how could it not? Nor did he blame her. But he had a job to do, part of which was getting the very best out of the vast talent in this group.

He leaned forward against his desk and peered into her stricken gaze. "This company needs you at your best." Then—he couldn't help himself—softer, "*I* need you at your best."

Rayne appeared to contemplate his words and drew her shoulders back. Something behind her eyes shifted. "You're right. I appreciate your honesty, Jack."

Good, girl. Jack sat back and smiled, until he realized he liked the sound of his name on her lips.

seven

A week after her meeting with Jack, Rayne leaned back in her chair and enjoyed the energy in the conference room filled with her creative design team colleagues. Everyone lounged in their chairs, relaxed, as they discussed the conceptual designs for their new project—a financial group headquartered in Dallas.

Jack sat at the head of the table, grinning as he flipped his pencil around. He was undeniably in his element managing this team. Rayne's gaze brushed over his crisp business shirt. Broad shoulders accentuated his lean physique. Warmth simmered against the collar of Rayne's blouse, and she quickly doused the wayward thought.

She could tell that everyone had accepted him. The women definitely loved him, especially Barb, who never missed an opportunity to flirt with him, though Rayne doubted it was intentional on Barb's part. Her friend simply didn't realize how she came across.

Rayne hoped.

At that moment, Barb spoke up. "You mentioned your plan for us to be more personally involved with the clients. That some of us would travel to the site. Will you be going as well?" Barb's eyes twinkled.

Oh brother.

Jack responded with a smile and the hint of something behind his eyes that Rayne couldn't read. "Initially."

More questions erupted about travel arrangements. Everyone seemed to be getting ahead of themselves, focusing on the benefits their new manager brought with him, rather than the purpose of the meeting—to brainstorm. She was interested to see how he would refocus their attention.

One question nagged her all morning during the meeting. How would they have felt toward her if she'd been named their manager? Jack's words about jealousy came to mind. Rayne fought to keep from frowning. He'd encouraged her to move past her regret at losing the promotion. Harold had probably made the right decision by bringing in someone outside of the company. But it certainly gave a person doubts about working her way up within this organization. She might have to go elsewhere in order to move up.

"All right, people. We've spent the morning going over this company and the image we want to portray. Let's not get off track with talk about travel." Jack stood and opened the door. Boxes of pizza floated into the room, the delivery guy hidden behind them. Jack lifted one of the stacks to help. "Or talk about pizza."

His comment elicited laughter.

"Consider this a working lunch. I want to hear your ideas. Let's get them on the table this afternoon without missing a beat."

Barb joined Jack in opening the pizza boxes then spreading them over the credenza behind the conference table, as well as the table itself. The receptionist entered, holding stacks of paper cups and plates.

Gail smiled at the delivery guy then addressed the design team. "Jack had me pick a variety, so I ordered pepperoni, supreme, cheese, Hawaiian, all meat, and vegetarian." She tugged large bottles of soda from a paper sack and set them on the table as well. "Now, if you don't mind, I'll just have a slice."

More chuckles resounded in the room as everyone grabbed paper plates or drinks and selected their slices of pizza.

"All this brain work burns a lot of calories," Simon said around a mouthful of Hawaiian pizza. "I'll have to eat twice as much now."

Rayne sat in her chair, watching. She'd wait until everyone got what they wanted then get her food. On the farm, when the men came in from the fields, they filled their plates first because they worked so hard during harvest and planting; then she and her mother ate what was left. For some reason, today's working lunch reminded her of those times. The habit of waiting had been instilled in her from an early age. She sighed.

Jack approached, carrying two plates filled with pizza. "What'll it be, Rayne? I think I've got one slice of every kind of pizza here."

He made her feel all warm inside. She smiled up at him. "I'll have cheese."

Jack slid into the chair next to her, ignoring the fact that someone else had been sitting there. "Working lunches can be like a shark feeding frenzy. If you don't jump into the fight, you might be left with nothing."

Rayne laughed. Should she share the reason she'd waited? Instead of replying, she took a bite of her pizza. It was hot, burning the top of her mouth, and she blew out a long breath, wishing she'd gotten some water. Jack hopped up and poured soda into a cup then handed it to her.

She took a quick drink. "Thank you." He was being far too attentive. From her peripheral vision, she could see Barb watching. Did Barb have designs on Jack?

While several conversations about the Dallas firm and fountain ideas buzzed around the room, Jack leaned toward Rayne and spoke softly. "You're up first after lunch. That's why I wanted you to eat now."

Rayne stared. "I'm up with what?"

"I want your first impressions, your ideas for the designs. Remember, Rayne, you're lead designer. I can give you the title, but it means nothing if you don't demonstrate your abilities. We need you to jumpstart the inspiration for the project."

Her nerves puddled at her feet. What were her artistic impressions about the project? Her thoughts had been focused on Jack as a manager.

When she didn't reply, Jack spoke again. "I have complete confidence in you."

How did she tell him that this wasn't how she worked? She couldn't think up designs in the middle of a crowded room. Ideas came to her when she was alone in her office, in the quiet of night, or on the farm. . . .

Rayne took another bite. Over time she'd learned to be creative on a consistent basis in order to do her job, not just when the muse decided to visit. Could she learn to become artistic and imaginative while others watched?

Rayne sighed. Jack had given her an opportunity. She swallowed hard.

She wouldn't blow it.

Gail appeared in the conference room again, this time holding a huge bouquet of roses. The room erupted.

"Who's the lucky girl?"

"Someone has an admirer."

The receptionist walked along the length of the table and came to stand in front of Rayne. Rayne glanced next to her and across the table. Who could they be for? But no women were sitting near Rayne at the moment.

Leaning forward, Gail carefully placed the roses in front of Rayne.

She gasped. "These can't be for me. There has to be a mistake." She stood, both embarrassed and surprised.

The room grew increasingly hot, and she fought her desire to look at Jack's expression. For a fleeting moment, she'd imagined him sending her roses.

Absurd!

"Well, girl, open the card." Gail took the liberty of snagging the small envelope from the bouquet. She handed it to Rayne.

Rayne glanced around the room. Everyone stared at her, except, well, Jack. He appeared engrossed with something on his laptop.

"I really. . .this is embarrassing. I'll open it in my office."

Gripping the small card, Rayne snatched up the roses and rushed them out of the conference room. Once in her office, she slammed the door behind her.

"Oh Paul, these had better not be from you." Paul had invited her to lunch a couple of weeks ago while in town, but she'd had too much work and turned him down.

She struggled to rip the small card open. The harder she tried, the less success she had. Finally, she cut it in half with scissors just as Barb entered her office.

"What are you doing? You'll destroy the card!"

Rayne pieced together the two halves of the card.

> *Enjoyed seeing you over the holidays. Can I take you to lunch while I'm in town?*
>
> *Paul*

Rayne blew out a frustrated breath, just short of growling. "Why did you send these?"

"Why did who send them?" Barb asked. "Tell me, Rayne."

Shrugging, Rayne let the card slip from her hand into the wastebasket. "An old friend and would-be suitor back home."

Barb gasped and rifled through the garbage, pulling out the card pieces. "I can't believe you would be so cold. This guy must really be into you. Is he that bad?"

Rayne huffed again and sank to her chair. "No, he's a nice guy. Good-looking, too." She looked up at Barb. "You'd like him."

"I don't understand. What's the problem?"

He's not Jack. Rayne felt her eyes grow wide, but at least the errant thought hadn't been spoken aloud. What had gotten into her? "I'm embarrassed that he sent these to me at work. And I just hope he's not harboring hope for something between us."

Apparently, he wasn't one to give up.

Still, she was touched by his gesture, if only slightly.

❧

Jack stood outside Rayne's door, his hand poised to knock.

He could hear the women talking inside. Footfalls resounded in the hallway. It would look like he was eavesdropping, but that wasn't his intention.

He didn't want to throw the door open like Harold, asserting himself, especially in this situation. Rayne had just received flowers; he should give her a moment. But he didn't want to lose the momentum of this morning by her disappearance.

He knocked softly on the door.

Barb snatched it open, her face spreading into a giant smile. "Oh, hi. Come in."

Her tone was light and flirtatious. Annoying.

Rayne's hands covered her face. She slowly let them drop in her lap.

Jack's throat grew tight. This was a good thing, really. She had an admirer, a boyfriend. Jack wouldn't have to be afraid of an emotional connection with her. He should rejoice.

The women stared at him. He should say something. He wanted to ask who the roses were from. But it wasn't his business. Completely inappropriate.

"Rayne, when you're ready. We need you back at the meeting." He grinned. "That is, if you can come down from cloud nine for a bit."

Rayne's lips flatlined. She shook her head. "It's not like that."

Jack threw up his hands. "It's not my concern."

He backed from the office, looking into Rayne's eyes. Though he shouldn't attempt to read her reaction to his comment, there it was.

Disappointment.

As he made his way to the conference room where the others finished up their lunch, Jack thought about what he'd seen in her eyes.

He had to be wrong, which meant he was losing his touch, unable to read people anymore. Or maybe he simply wasn't able to read Rayne.

Later that afternoon, Jack was relieved to be alone in his office. The rest of the meeting did not go as planned, at least for him. Rayne gave her initial impressions of their newest client, as Jack had requested she do. But the energy present during the morning hours had dissipated.

Flowers. How could a bouquet of roses disrupt his thoughts? He could tell that Rayne had become distracted as well.

Hands jammed in his pockets, he tried to peer through the glass, but it had grown too dark outside, and all he could see was his own frayed reflection. He kicked over the wastebasket.

Rayne's familiar laughter in the hallway penetrated his door. Who had given her the roses? Why should he care?

He scraped the paper back into the wastebasket and set it right, then blew out a frustrated breath. Opening his door, he peered down the hall. Rayne leaned against the wall outside her office, chatting with Heidi, one of the techies, if he remembered correctly.

He would have stepped back into his office, but Heidi spotted him.

"Hi, Jack. Are we making too much noise?" she asked with a smile.

"No, not at all. Just wondered who was working late, that's all." Jack meandered toward the women.

Rayne looked away from him.

Jack felt a wry grin slip into his lips. How was it that others in the company offered him warm smiles, but Rayne always seemed detached when he was around? Moments before, he'd heard her laughter. It was nice.

But he was done with love and relationships, so her reaction to him shouldn't bother him in the least. He didn't care about the roses either. Jack was back, all about the job.

Heidi cleared her throat. "I was just about to leave. Rayne is going ice-skating with me. Would you like to go?"

Rayne lifted her eyes to Jack. "Heidi's going with her church group. It's their couple's night. So unless you have a significant other, you might feel uncomfortable."

She studied him, a question in her gaze.

Jack's throat constricted again. Rayne was probably going with her secret admirer.

Heidi squeezed Rayne's arm. "It really makes no difference. Sure, we're getting together, but anyone can come. Rayne's coming, and she's single. How about it, Jack?"

Jack grinned. "I've never been ice-skating." He scratched his chin.

Heidi smiled. "Well, maybe it's time to change that."

eight

Rayne skated to the side of the outdoor rink—part of the new park in Fargo—and grabbed the wall, feeling winded. When she was younger, ice-skating had been a favorite pastime. That and snowmobiling.

Heidi skated over to her and put her hand on the rail. "There's a good crowd here tonight."

"Thank goodness. It's easier to skate in a crowd—nobody pays attention to the clumsy skater."

Heidi laughed. "You mean like Jack?" She gestured with her head.

On the other side of the rink, Jack tumbled on the ice.

Heidi laughed. "Poor guy."

"Why on earth did you invite him?"

"Oh come on. I was trying to be friendly. You might try it sometime."

Rayne yanked her gaze from Jack to give Heidi a questioning look.

She lifted her mouth in a huge grin. "You know I'm only kidding. But why don't you go over and give the guy a hand?"

"I still can't figure out why he came." Rayne could hardly stand to watch him struggle. "He's like a little kid out there."

"Adorable."

Rayne wouldn't step up to the bait. "He's not allowed to be adorable. He's my boss."

"So what? Look at Carissa and John. They met at work."

Rayne wasn't going to fall for what appeared to be another matchmaking scheme. Heidi was happily married and had a child. Married women with children wanted everyone else to know what they were missing. Heidi had made an attempt at matchmaking for Rayne a few months ago.

It didn't work then. *And it won't work now.*

Heidi's husband, Jim, skated up and into her. She squealed and they laughed, pushing away from the wall together. "See you later, Rayne."

As Rayne shoved off as well, deciding this would be her last go-around, she discovered she was next to Jack. "You're doing much better," she said.

He cautiously took his eyes from the ice to glance at her. "You think?"

She couldn't help but smile. Heidi was right. He was adorable. And Barb was right; he was beautiful. "I think."

"You should see me on the racquetball court. I'm much better."

"Racquetball, huh? I don't think I've ever played that."

Jack opened his mouth; then. . .he was on his back.

Rayne stopped. "Ow! That had to hurt."

Wincing, he sat on the ice and looked up at her. "I have no idea why I even came."

Rayne pressed her lips together to keep from laughing. She was actually beginning to feel sorry for the guy. "Here, let me help you up." She offered her gloved hand.

He arched his left brow. "Are you sure about that?"

Rayne braced her legs and gripped the ice with her skates. "Of course."

He thrust his hand into hers and tugged.

Rayne's skates slipped as the wall seemed to fly past. Pain met her backside. She looked over at Jack. He smiled.

She erupted in laughter, and then Jack joined her. She smacked him on the arm. "You did that on purpose."

"You think?"

Warmth spread through her despite the cold. "I think."

"I needed your help. I didn't think I could get up one more time."

Skates scraped the ice. Heidi and Jim stood over them. "You two would look cozier if you were sitting in front of a fire."

Rayne glared at Heidi. "Help me up, would you?"

"And end up on the ice with you? No thanks." Heidi and Jim skated away, holding hands.

"Of all the—"

Jack scrambled to his feet, and before Rayne could do the same, he gripped her arms and lifted her up with hardly any effort. The man was strong. He brushed the snow off her shoulders.

A few snowflakes stuck in his dark hair. Rayne wanted to brush them off, as he'd done for her, but she feared she'd end up running her fingers through. Of course, to get the full effect, she'd have to remove her gloves. Her eyes widened. What was she thinking?

Jack stared at her expectantly; then with a half grin, he said, "I think I'm done. Good night, Rayne."

"Good night," she said. As she watched him skate over to the exit door, Rayne didn't want him to leave. Not yet.

She'd just welcomed the fact that he was here. Skating around the rink, she stepped off the ice and saw Jack enter a warming hut. She followed him and, once inside, spotted him tugging off his skates.

"Hi there," she said.

He pulled off a skate and peered up at her.

"Mind if I join you?" she asked.

After tugging off his other skate, he sat tall. "Not at all. I'm about to leave, though."

"Why did you come to skate when you don't know how? It must have been torture." *What are you doing, girl?*

"You mean embarrassing." He hung his head then looked up at her.

He had the most amazing eyes. "True." She giggled.

"I don't know. I guess I wanted to get to know a few people. I'm new to Fargo, you know?"

"Heidi attends a great church. You should try it sometime. You'll get to know people there. Make friends."

"Is that where you attend?"

Rayne stared at him. Why did he want to know?

"She's invited me, and I've visited a few times, but I'm just so accustomed to the church I grew up in, it's tough finding someplace new, fitting in."

Jack studied Rayne. She shivered. For a moment, she wished he would tug her to him, warming her.

"Listen, I noticed an ice sculpture on display in the park. Thought I'd go check it out. Want to come with me?" he asked.

Two men came into the warming hut, followed by several kids. "It's getting crowded in here. Sounds like a good idea. I have to get my shoes first."

After putting her shoes on and returning her skates, Rayne found Jack waiting for her next to the ice rink. "There you are," she said.

He pointed to the other side of the rink. "The sculpture is over there."

Rayne tugged her coat tighter. "The snow is beginning to fall heavier now."

As they trudged side by side through the snow, couples and families walked nearby, many heading to their cars, ending their fun evening. For some reason, Rayne felt self-conscious that so many held hands. She almost felt as though she and Jack should hold hands if they wanted to fit in. But how many others were walking in the park with their boss?

Rayne stopped. Heidi and Jim stood next to their car in a romantic hug. Then Heidi tilted her head up, and Jim met her with a kiss.

Shaking off the scene, Rayne continued to walk. She glanced over at Jack.

He was watching her. "What's bothering you?"

"Nothing. I'm fine." What could she say? *"You're my boss, and I can't hold your hand"*?

"Here it is." Jack put his gloved hands under his arms, shivering.

The ice sculpture appeared to be an abstract of a flock of geese.

Rayne sent him a sympathetic smile. "You look so miserable."

"I'm from Florida. But I ended up in Southern Cal when I went to work for Disney. I prefer it hot—what do you expect?"

Rayne nodded her head in an exaggerated manner. "Right."

Jack laughed. "Tell me what you see."

"What? In this sculpture?"

"Yes."

"I think you've got me wrong. I only do fluid water sculptures."

Jack threw his head back and laughed. Rayne thought it was the most delightful thing she'd ever heard.

28.

Rayne was. . .Jack shook his head. There was just something about her. "So, she has a sense of humor, after all."

She grinned—a beautiful grin—and shook her head. "Listen, it's been a long day. I'm tired and cold to the bone. Do I really have to turn on the creativity right now?"

"You don't have to. This isn't work."

Rayne circled the sculpture. "I'm standing next to a water sculpture, ice sculpture, rather, with my boss who wants to know my impression. How is that not work?"

Jack wanted to run his hand down the sculpture, but the sign warned people from touching it. How to answer her question. . . ? He rubbed his gloved fingers over his face. His lips must be blue by now.

"I don't know, Rayne. It doesn't feel like work to me." From across the circle, he stared at her, trying to read her expression. *Maybe because you fascinate me.*

"I'm sorry if I didn't seem focused enough this afternoon during the brainstorming meeting."

"Well, you did just receive a bouquet of roses. I'm sure any woman would be starry-eyed after that. What can a boss expect?" Ugh. Had he actually brought up the roses? He thought he'd convinced himself he didn't care who had sent them.

Rayne reached toward the ice sculpture as if she planned to touch it, then drew back. "The flowers. . .it's not like that. I mean, the guy who sent the roses is someone from back home who can't let go."

At her news, pressure seemed to ease from Jack's chest. Had he really held on to hope that the flowers had meant nothing to her?

He shouldn't even care. His stomach soured when thoughts of his previous broken engagement deposited a snowdrift of unwanted memories in his mind. "Go easy on the guy, okay? I know what it feels like to be hurt in love." Jack shivered. Why had he revealed that to her?

He chuckled, embarrassed. When he glanced up at Rayne again, a soft smile caressed her lips. Maybe she was just too easy to talk to and he'd allowed himself to get too comfortable with her.

"I think the cold is getting to you." Rayne trotted around the sculpture and grabbed Jack's arm. "Come on."

"What are you doing? Where are we going?"

"You like it hot?" She giggled. "Then there's nothing better than hot chocolate on a cold night like this."

Jack snapped out of it. She was right—the cold had numbed his brain. "You should probably get home before the roads get too messy."

"Oh, really? Remember, I have lived in the North my entire life. I know how to drive in this, unlike others who come from the sunny, warm states." Rayne laughed.

Jack grinned, liking that she'd loosened up, cast off that professional veneer for him. It was nice having her not think of him as her boss all the time.

But then, what was he doing?

Concern jabbed him, taunting him. *Are you nuts, man?*

"No, really. You need to get home and warm. Maybe you're not worried about driving in this, but I am."

She slowed and released his arm, turning to face him. Her expression grew sober. Oh how he wished he would have kept his mouth shut.

"You're serious, aren't you?"

"Let me walk you to your car," he said. Rayne acted as if she might resist at first, but she let him hold her gloved hand. In the parking lot, Jack searched the few cars left. "Let me guess."

He glanced at Rayne to see where she was looking, but she stared at the dark sky, smiling. "I'm not going to give you any clues. And you'd better get it right."

"Let's see. Which car would a creative and beautiful woman like Rayne Flemming drive?" Boy, had he dug himself in deep with this one.

Jack tugged Rayne behind him as they walked past cars. A gold Toyota Camry, a black Prius, a red Hyundai Sonata. Jack enjoyed holding her hand and having her near him. He stopped, unwilling to take the test. "I can't. I have no idea."

He turned to see her expression. She smiled a simple, sweet smile; then her lips parted just so, seeming to beg him to kiss them. Her eyes slid shut. At that moment, he almost answered the tug on his heart and pressed his lips against hers.

Her lids fluttered open. "I. . .uh. . .Jack," she whispered his name.

He'd already decided he loved the way she said his name. He leaned in, but wait. . . . *What are you doing, man?*

She backed against the door of a white VW Passat. "This is it, Jack. You found my car."

nine

Jack shoved the door to his apartment closed behind him and shook his hair over the tiled entryway, dumping snow. He brushed off his shoulders—should have done it outside, but he was too cold to care. He shrugged out of his coat and gloves, thinking he'd need to buy a cap to keep the warmth from seeping out of his head.

Tomorrow he'd be sore, all right, from all the falling. He hurried to the kitchen and turned on the stovetop to warm his hands. Rayne was right—hot chocolate was a great idea.

Part of him wished he would have shared it with her. Thankfully, he'd come to his senses before he'd done something crazy like kiss her. That would have been a quick way out of a job. She'd given him no indication of her interest—at least not in so many words. Feeling the blood flow back in his hands, he poured cocoa mix into a cup of water and stuck it in the microwave.

Then there was the matter of his pact with himself. After what had happened last year, he could never give his heart to someone—the risk was too great.

Too wound up to sleep, he sipped on the hot chocolate while watching a comedy and unpacking a few remaining boxes. Originally he'd planned to leave a few things boxed so that when he finally bought a house, he wouldn't have to repack.

But that side of his life wasn't on his fast-track plan. Might as well get cozy in the apartment for a while. He laughed at a comical scene playing on the TV as he cut open a box and looked inside.

She stared at him.

Jack stumbled back. Who had packed that picture of her?

He knew he hadn't done it. Jack rubbed his eyes, thinking back to the week he moved. Several of his buddies in San Diego had helped him pack. All of them knew that she was the reason he left the company.

And now it was as though she laughed at him, laughed at his cold misery, and reminded him of why he would never love anyone else. Loving a woman gave her too much power over you.

Jack groused at himself for his melodrama. He tugged the framed photo from the box and considered that he hadn't thought about her much over the last several weeks. No, he'd been thinking about someone else.

The picture was one of Kiera's best. She'd given it to him on his birthday—so sure he'd want to see her every day. Luscious golden hair tumbled over her shoulders. Stunning eyes—made even more striking with mascara and shadow—stared back at him. Perfect lips opened into a sensual smile—just for him.

He closed his eyes, feeling dizzy with anger.

She'd toyed with him. They looked good as a couple, she'd said. But her heart wasn't in it—did she even have a heart?

Jack sank onto the sofa, ignoring the television and the neighbor next door who banged on the wall for him to turn the volume down.

Rayne was the exact opposite of Kiera—Rayne was beautiful where it counted. She was real.

Stumbling from the couch over to the kitchen, he pressed the lever on the garbage can and dropped Kiera's picture into the container, putting her where she belonged.

And as for Rayne? She worked for him. End of story.

He loved what he was doing at FountainTech. Why risk everything again?

He turned his focus to his new invention.

❧

For the next several weeks, Rayne worked with the design team members to translate their designs into the 3-D model on the computer, and from there, once they were satisfied with the results, they entered the creation into the software. Their special software would then control the pumps and nozzles, resulting in a water fountain. Jack told her that the magic all started with her as lead designer, and then continued with her ability to translate all the ideas into something that could be visualized.

She hadn't worked much with Jack at all, which concerned her, considering he'd given her creative lead and made certain she understood they would work closely together. But she'd hardly seen him since the night they'd gone ice-skating.

Rayne stared at the computer screen and then hung her head.

Jack was out of town this week with Barb, visiting the customer site to fine-tune details of the project. As creative lead, Rayne knew she should have gone with him. He hadn't invited her. She sensed he'd built a great divide between them—but perhaps that was her overactive imagination—as if there were, in fact, any reason for him to distance himself from her.

She stood tall and stretched her back, needing some fresh coffee to jolt her out of this melancholy. One of the problems with being an artistic person was the tendency toward extremes. She was either flying high, soaring with the eagles, or her mood was deep in a cave with the bats.

And right now that cave was looming just ahead of her.

Rayne strode down the hall to the kitchen, offering half smiles to coworkers here and there as she passed. Turning the corner that would take her to the kitchen, she bumped into Terry, a man she rarely saw on this floor.

He sloshed coffee all over himself and winced, then glared down at her.

"Oh, I'm so sorry. Let me get you a towel."

"No, that's all right. I'll take care of this in the men's room." He trotted off in a huff.

The incident reminded her of the first time she met Jack. Rayne sighed, pouring herself a cup of coffee. They really should have put her office somewhere else to keep her from running into people. She needed to focus when she approached the kitchen.

She laughed to herself, glad she was alone. As she left the kitchen, she decided she missed Barb, and. . .she missed Jack.

Back in her office, she stared out the window, unable to concentrate on the fountain. The snow had finally let up, and the sun beat down on Fargo, though the temperature was still below freezing.

Once Jack returned, he wouldn't be impressed with her anymore.

When he'd chosen Barb to accompany him on the trip, he'd sucked all the creativity out of Rayne. Barb had a thing for Jack. He had to know that, and going on a business trip with her might be dangerous for him, especially with the way Barb flirted with him. That is, if Jack wanted to avoid an office romance, Barb would be hard to resist. She was beautiful—the kind of woman who could easily catch any man's attention. Who was she kidding?

She was jealous of Barb. The woman had a right to like Jack. Who was Rayne to say she didn't?

Rayne plopped in her chair, feeling anything but inspired about this fountain.

She was losing her touch.

That night at the ice-skating rink, Rayne had been sure Jack was going to kiss her. She closed her eyes, remembering how she felt, how she longed to feel his arms around her, but they had both snatched themselves from the magic moment. Or could it have all been in her head alone?

That had to be it—Jack had seen that she had feelings for him, knew that's why she had tried to be aloof around him and failed. That's why Jack had appeared reserved around her.

Her emotions and his actions could be a huge detriment to the client. Harold would see that this team wasn't producing as well as it did before Jack came on board.

And that would be all Rayne's fault.

How did one escape romantic tension in the workplace? Maybe this was a sign from God. She couldn't work in this environment.

With Jack.

Her office phone rang.

Jack!

Heart pounding, she answered. Gail told Rayne that a Craig Hammerman was on the line. Rayne wasn't familiar with the name, but she took the call anyway, feeling the fool for wishing Jack would call her. She had to nix these fantasies.

"This is Rayne Flemming."

"My name is Craig Hammerman. I'm a headhunter, and I have a company very interested in your talents."

Rayne held her breath, trying to comprehend what she'd just heard. "I'm not interested."

"Miss Flemming. It would be worth your while to hear me out. Get all the facts before you make your decision."

"I. . .I don't know."

"This company is very similar to FountainTech, only working in a different market niche entirely. You would manage a team of designers. I can promise you a better salary than you're making now."

Rayne shook her head. "How did you get my number?"

"You mean, how do I know about you? Let's just say my client is aware of your designs."

"Where is the company located?"

"I can't give you that information just yet. But it's not in North Dakota."

"I'll have to get back to you. Give me your number."

"Miss Flemming, this opportunity is short-lived. There are other designers being considered. Don't think too long."

Rayne wrote down the phone number and said good-bye. She drew in a deep breath then exhaled. Just a few short weeks ago the news that she'd lost the promotion to Jack had almost devastated her. For so long, she'd planned to work her way up and show her family that she was meant for the business world. For so long, she wished she could put aside the hold they held over her—but it wasn't that easy.

To some extent, thanks to Jack, she'd been able to put the loss behind her. In a short period of time, he'd earned her loyalty. Still, didn't she owe it to herself to consider this new opportunity? And she'd already decided Jack's fountain would be better without her, considering her misplaced feelings toward him.

"When opportunity knocks, and you walk through that door, just remember it comes with a price. Count the cost." Though she'd left the farm, her father's words of wisdom were never far away.

༚

Jack leaned his head against the seat back, feeling the pressure against his body as the jet took off. He closed his eyes, relieved that this trip would finally end.

Barb sat quietly next to him, flipping through a magazine she'd tugged from the seat back in front of her.

He pinched the bridge of his nose. Rayne should have been the one with him. The client would have been amazed with her perceptiveness and her impressions. Instead, he'd brought a Barbie doll. The woman was talented, too, but it wasn't the same.

And her focus was off. Though she was professional in every way that counted, he could tell that she had romantic notions about him. All he could do was ignore her subtle overtures. The tension brought to light his own emotions where Rayne was concerned.

Was that the reason Rayne had acted standoffish toward him? Had she sensed something from him and consequently felt trapped by her boss? He slid his hand down his face and groaned. Oh, he hoped not.

"What's bothering you, Jack?"

Jack opened his eyes. Barb was still flipping through the magazine. "Oh, I could really use one of those"—she pointed at a massage gizmo—"since I don't have anyone at home to rub my back."

Jack shut his eyes again. Barb was an exotic beauty.

Like Kiera.

Any other normal red-blooded man would struggle against the temptation she offered. But Kiera had cured him. Utterly.

Simon would have been a better choice on this trip, but then Jack would have had to listen to him comparing himself to Rayne.

Rayne. . .

"Jack." Someone tugged on his arm.

He opened his eyes and squinted. Where was he? Oh right, the flight back from Dallas to Fargo.

Barb's sensual perfume drew him fully awake.

"Hey there, you're awake now." Barb leaned in close to whisper in his ear. "You said someone's name in your sleep. I promise to keep it just between you and me."

Stunned, he couldn't respond. Had he said Rayne's name? He'd had a dream about her.

He turned his head, despite the danger in Barb's proximity, to read her eyes.

A slight smile quirked the right side of her lovely mouth. She looked pleased with herself.

"Barb," she whispered. "You said my name."

ten

"Ow!" Rayne jerked her hand back from the hot roaster, nearly dropping the pan as she slid it onto the stove. Nudging the oven door shut with her foot, she took one step across the small kitchen to the sink and ran her wrist under cold water, thinking she could just stick it out the window instead.

She laughed at her attempt at humor. She usually spent Friday evenings in a tired daze on the sofa, resting up from the week. Tonight she wished she'd taken Heidi up on her offer to join her at some church event.

Removing the roaster lid, she picked at the meat with a fork to see if it was tender like her mother's.

Tough as leather. Would she ever learn to cook?

She lifted a piece on the fork and blew on it to cool it off, then stuck it in her mouth, prepared to chew the leather, but it was impossible.

Opening the pantry, she grabbed a box of macaroni and cheese. What she needed at the moment was comfort food. Unable to get her mind off her lack of enthusiasm for the fountain she was charged with creating, or the fact that Jack and Barb had been gallivanting around Dallas this week, Rayne had decided to create a home-cooked meal, a reminder of home.

But she'd failed.

As she brought the water to a boil for the macaroni, Rayne decided she was about to fail again. She stared at her cell phone on the counter, dying to call Barb.

Fear stayed her hand. What would Barb say? Would she talk about the client and her experience, or would her conversation be filled with little details about her time with Jack?

Rayne poured the macaroni into the water and watched

it boil. A few minutes later her cell rang, just as the water boiled over onto the counter. This wasn't her night to cook.

She flipped open her cell. "This is Rayne."

"Rayne, it's Paul."

"Hi, Paul." Rayne frowned. The day after she'd received the roses, Paul had called to invite her to lunch, but she'd been in a meeting all day again.

"I'm in Fargo this weekend."

"What are you doing in town so often these days?" Rayne wasn't sure she wanted to know but asked before she thought.

"I'd love to tell you all about it. Have breakfast with me?"

Rayne weaved her fingers through her hair. She had no excuse. "Sure. What time?"

"Seven o'clock too early on a Saturday?"

At that, Rayne laughed. Growing up on a farm, she was more than familiar with the fact that things didn't come to a stop for the weekend. "That's fine."

"Great, I'll pick you up at seven."

"Uh, Paul. . .I'll just meet you." Rayne turned the stove off and moved the macaroni aside. It was going to be mushy. She hated mushy macaroni and cheese.

Paul was silent for a moment. "Have any place in mind?"

She'd disappointed him. A sick feeling hit her stomach. "Martha's Waffle House just off Main."

"I'll be there."

"Looking forward to it." Rayne snapped the phone shut and leaned against the counter. She cared for Paul, and, she admitted, there was a small part of her that still found him very attractive. After all, she'd dated him and had come close to marrying him.

She'd never been one to date much in high school or college—only two boyfriends and one other admirer. It was a vicious cycle—liking someone who liked someone else. If the world were perfect, would she be able to return Paul's feelings, loving him with abandon?

In a perfect world, she'd have no feelings for Jack.

The next morning, Rayne shoved through the glass doors of Martha's Waffle House and stood in the small foyer, looking around the restaurant for Paul. She'd seen his truck outside.

There. He waved his arm, catching her attention.

She hadn't wanted to meet him this morning, but she didn't seem to have an out. He was a family friend. If nothing else, a neighbor, just taking her to breakfast. Sliding into the booth across from him, she smiled, hating the shy feeling that came over her as though she was his date. She'd spent enough time romantically involved with him that she too easily slipped back into the role.

"I took the liberty of ordering coffee for you." Paul's lips curved into a grin, and he winked. "I know you love your coffee."

"Thanks." Rayne poured some into her cup from the carafe then looked at Paul. He'd always been a considerate man. With his piercing blue eyes and blond Norwegian look, what woman wouldn't fall over herself to go out with him, or. . .marry him?

They ordered breakfast. After the failed attempt at her mother's cooking and the mushy macaroni, Rayne was famished.

"So, what are you doing in Fargo?" she asked.

"I'm selling the farm, Rayne." He studied her.

She sucked in a breath. He'd landed a punch to her stomach. "But. . .why?" The words fairly croaked from her. She'd had no clue that she could even care so much.

"I want something else for my life. I've been looking for a job here in Fargo."

Confusion flooded Rayne's heart and showed in her expression, she was sure. She welcomed the plate of food—steak and eggs—the waitress placed before her, coupled with a fresh carafe of hot coffee.

Rayne inhaled deeply. "What are you doing, Paul? The farm is who you are."

Paul finished smothering his short stack with butter and syrup. He looked up from his work of art at Rayne, giving her a stare filled with hurt. "Oh, so I'm forever relegated to be a farmer in your eyes?"

Rayne shook her head, chewing her eggs. She swallowed. What was he really trying to say? That he wanted to work in Fargo so that he would be more appealing to her? How could she make him understand?

But maybe he was right. Rayne couldn't see past the farmer in Paul. She took a sip of her coffee and shut her eyes, recalling memories of her time with Paul when they were growing up. An image of him sliding into the mud, unable to stand without slipping once again came to mind.

Rayne grinned. "Do you remember when you were stuck in the mud?"

"And you came to my rescue, only you ended up just as muddy as me?"

While they ate breakfast, Rayne and Paul reminisced about the good times and the bad times they'd had together on neighboring farms. For Rayne it was easier to slip into discussing happy memories, and she sensed the same from Paul. Talking about their past was safer than talking about the future. At times in her life, she considered him her best friend. What had happened? Why had she drifted away?

Why had she wanted more?

The price for pursuing her dream seemed to be leaving behind the people she loved, leaving behind the security of what she knew. Leaving behind so much of herself, of who she was.

Rayne looked from her plate, where her food was quickly disappearing, and into Paul's eyes, feeling herself warmed by his company. She'd forgotten moments like these when she enjoyed being with him. She was glad she came after all.

Paul reached across the table and took her hand, startling her. Her hand was so small in his large, calloused one. Did she feel a spark, or was it simply warm familiarity that she welcomed? Her hand in his seemed to magnify the lonely ache in her heart. From the look in his eyes, she feared they were back to what Paul really wanted to discuss with her.

"Rayne, I've watched you pursue your dream. You seem happy enough. If you can do it, then maybe I need to be bold enough to step away from the farm. You're my inspiration."

She slipped her hand from his. "Oh Paul, I can't say that I'm happy. Right now I'm more confused than anything." With all the stress and pressure at work lately, Rayne longed to be curled in her warm bed at the farmhouse, the smell of bacon and eggs wafting up from the kitchen in the early morning. Though the farming life was marked with long and laborious days, Rayne almost missed it now.

"If I lived here in Fargo, had a job; if I weren't a farmer. . ."

Pain sliced through her. Was he actually considering selling the farm, thinking that it would make a difference? She hoped not—that would be too big a burden for her to carry.

Rayne fell back against the booth, fearing the rest of his question. "But, Paul, you *are* a farmer. I can't see you as anything else."

Pain flooded his expression, the creases in his brow and around his mouth making him look much older.

This time Rayne was the one to reach across the table. She placed her hand over his and pressed gently. What Paul did for his livelihood had nothing to do with how she felt. But at the moment, she knew those words would fall cruelly if she said them, crushing him further.

Speaking softly, Rayne said, "I don't think you would be happy doing anything else. That's all I meant."

Finally, they fell to reminiscing again and talked until there was nothing more to say. Paul ushered her out of the restaurant to her car, and she hoped he wouldn't invite her to spend more time with him today. Being with him, all the good memories seemed to surface, making her miserable with the choices she'd made.

He smiled down at her. "Thank you for having breakfast with me today, Rayne. I've missed you."

"I've missed you, too." She smiled, startled by her feelings. Her gut twisted. Though true, she shouldn't have spoken her thoughts.

Before she knew what was happening, Paul leaned down and pressed his lips against hers, lingering. Rayne allowed the kiss, trying to draw something from it. But what—an answer?

When Paul pulled back, he ran the back of his hand down her cheek. "Come home, Rayne."

"Oh Paul. . ." *If only you knew.*

Tears blurred her vision. Rayne's heart was traitorous, betraying him with thoughts of Jack. Betraying Jack with thoughts of Paul.

❧

On Sunday morning, Jack rolled over, flopping his arm across his bed, and groaned. He'd just had a terrible dream in which he'd kissed Barb. A nightmare. With one squinting eye, he peered at the clock on the nightstand. Nine thirty.

What time did Heidi's church start? Jack rubbed his eyes, his face, and his chin then stared at the ceiling. He'd liked the few people he'd met from her church that night he'd joined them at the ice-skating rink. Would Rayne be there?

Jack crawled from bed, yawning, and stumbled to the bathroom where he brushed his teeth in an attempt to remove any remnant of the Barb-kissing dream. Had the woman somehow planted her spores in him? She was like a bad taste in his mouth that he couldn't seem to get out. In fact, he could still smell the scent of her perfume.

Searching his room, he grabbed the clothes he'd thrown over a chair—her perfume still clinging to them because he'd sat next to her on the plane—and threw them into the hamper where they should have gone in the first place.

There was no way—*no way*—he'd said her name while sleeping on the plane. Why would she claim he had?

If anything, he should have said Rayne's name, because he'd thought often of the moment he'd almost kissed her.

Could he actually have said Rayne's name? Not good. The idea that he wasn't in control of any facet of his life, even dreaming, scared him.

Shaking off the thoughts, he made coffee, and while it brewed, he showered and dressed.

Scrambling eggs, he thought about the fountain models he'd seen yesterday. A few days away from the office left him feeling unsure about how the project was progressing. Anxious to see what Rayne had come up with, he'd gone into the office and looked at her computer models of the fountain.

Something was missing from her design. Jack knew it took more than one person to create a water sculpture, but he also knew that Rayne had more to give than she put into the model.

Substandard work wasn't acceptable on Jack's team. Joining FountainTech, he felt like his yacht had finally come in, but right now it was springing a lot of little leaks, one of which was Barb. Why couldn't he take this company where he wanted it go to without people issues?

Jack blew out a breath. As he had told Rayne, there would always be office politics—the human element. He'd been avoiding Rayne because he had to stanch the flow of feelings he had for her, and now he would have to avoid Barb because she apparently liked him. Jack had not prepared for these types of obstacles in his plan for creating the world's best water sculptures. He couldn't very well call Barb on her lack of professionalism, because he had the same problem. At least he was that honest.

Thankfully, his eggs were done. He had twenty minutes to eat and make it to Heidi's church, which started at ten thirty. After finishing his breakfast, he pulled the curtains back and stared out at the snow-laden landscape. Another gray, empty day lay ahead of him.

It reminded him of his life. He chugged the rest of his coffee to warm his insides, but the warmth couldn't penetrate deep enough. At that moment, Jack recognized that something was missing in his life. He sensed it, just like he'd sensed something amiss in Rayne's design. But what was it?

He tugged on his coat and mentally prepared himself to step into the cold. Then he knew what was missing. . . .

Jack stepped outside into the frigid North Dakota air. The day was gray and cloudy, devoid of light. Just like his soul.

He followed the directions he'd found on the Fargo Community Church Web site. He couldn't recall the last time he'd been out and about on a Sunday morning. Traffic was minimal, offering a stress-free and peaceful drive. If he wasn't on his way to church, he might enjoy taking in the scenery.

But he was a man on a twofold mission. This morning he was missing two things in his life, though he wasn't completely prepared to admit to either. Feeling as if he had an enormous, dark cavern inside, he recognized that he might need to exercise some spiritual muscle if he wanted to get in shape. After all, he went to the gym and played racquetball to keep himself physically healthy. Any idiot had to know that the same held true for the inside of a person.

He'd been an idiot for too long already.

Jack pressed against the seat back, not certain he was ready for this.

At least he was taking a first step in going to church, right? If he was recalling it correctly, there was a saying that went, "The journey of a thousand miles begins with a single step." He hoped that God could see that he was at least making an effort.

Just outside of Fargo, Jack began scanning the roadside. There. The Fargo Community Church sign seemed to smile at him from the left side of the road. After waiting for a truck to pass, he turned into the parking lot and drove slowly, looking for an empty spot. His palms grew sweaty against the steering wheel, especially when people stared at him as they headed across the parking lot toward the church. They must be curious about the visitor.

Maybe this wasn't such a good idea.

Jack found a parking spot near the exit. Good. He could leave quickly if needed. Swiping his hands down his slacks, he tugged on his gloves for the short jaunt to the church doors. Someone opened one of the double doors for him as he approached, and he rushed through, uttering his thanks through white, cloudy breath.

The gentleman offered him a church bulletin and silently pointed toward the sanctuary. Someone was already speaking to the gathering, so Jack slipped in and, after spotting a vacant place in a pew, crept over to the space. A family with three small children peered at him, the mother smiling as one of her children crawled onto her lap.

A quick scan of the large room told him there were about two hundred people attending. While the man at the pulpit gave the announcements, Jack perused the bulletin, hoping to ignore the inquisitive stares, but he really wanted to look around himself. Was Rayne here?

He should have thought to look for her car.

Guilt slid around his neck, tightening, because he knew that Rayne shouldn't be his reason for going to church. Feeling the heat, Jack realized he'd not removed his coat and attempted to slip out of it without drawing too much attention. While he did, he took the opportunity to gaze around the church, searching.

He caught the back of Heidi's head near the front, he thought. A few other familiar faces from when he'd gone ice-skating were scattered throughout the sanctuary. Recognizing a few of the congregants gave him a measure of peace, and he relaxed against the pew, ready to listen.

Except, where was Rayne?

A lively tune sprang from the band up front; then everyone stood. Jack followed suit, and though he only knew a few of the songs, he did his best to fit in. After what seemed to

Jack like an eternity, the worship ended and the gathering took its seats once again.

From the bulletin, Jack learned that Pastor Luke would be preaching today. Jack frowned, remembering that he should have brought a Bible. Fortunately, the church kept a copy of the book in the racks on the pews. He tugged a New American Standard Bible from the back of the pew in front of him and opened it up to 1 Samuel 16.

Jack couldn't seem to wipe the frown from his face. He really missed Rayne, wanted—no, needed—to see her this morning. Could he ignore his disappointment long enough to hear the sermon?

Pastor Luke told the story about how God chose a shepherd boy to rule over Israel while he was yet a small boy. God overlooked his older brothers to choose the youngest and most insignificant of Jesse's gang because God looks at the heart.

The pastor read from 1 Samuel 16:7. " 'But the Lord said to Samuel, "Do not look at his appearance or at the height of his stature, because I have rejected him; for God sees not as man sees, for man looks at the outward appearance, but the Lord looks at the heart." ' "

Jack rubbed his chin, considering the words. What exactly did God see in Jack's heart? He wasn't sure he wanted to know the answer. So far, over the years, ignoring the pain he felt inside had worked for him. That is, until this morning.

As he allowed the words to sink deeper, he thought of Rayne. Again. Whatever attracted him to her, he knew, came from what was inside her. What was in her heart.

The realization made him smile. He was deep in thought when the church service finally ended and he stood, gathering his coat. The couple next to him shook his hand and welcomed him.

"Jack, so good to see you here." Heidi reached across the pew between them to grab his hand. With her other hand, she gripped the smaller fingers of a beautiful little girl with blond curls and Heidi's soft green eyes.

He smiled back at Heidi and the little girl, who he assumed was her daughter. "I'm glad I came," he said, and glanced over Heidi's head, searching the dispersing crowd.

"I'm guessing that you're looking for Rayne." An amused smile played on her lips.

He pinned her with his gaze. "And what makes you say that?"

"Are you denying it?"

Jack laughed. "I guess I can't hide anything from you."

Heidi ran her palm over her daughter's hair, affection in her gaze. "She's not here. Maybe if she knows you're coming, she'll come, too."

"I don't know if that's the right reason for anyone to go to church, is it?" he asked, a frown grazing his lips. Hadn't he come in part to see Rayne?

Heidi sighed. "No, but in Rayne's case, she often drives all the way out to her old church. She has such deep roots there, it's hard for her to let go and find a new church family."

"I see." Jack stuck the Bible into the back of the pew. "It was nice to see you, Heidi."

"You, too, Jack." Heidi's attentions were quickly drawn away by her little girl.

Sweet. What would it be like to have a wife and child of his own? If he married Rayne, would their daughter have Rayne's infinitely thoughtful eyes?

A longing gushed through him. Coming to church today hadn't solved anything, but instead seemed to magnify the hole in his life. Now the emptiness had become a gaping abyss.

A sudden thirst gripped Jack, and he headed to the water fountain. He strongly suspected this thirst couldn't be quenched with water.

eleven

Monday morning, Rayne perused the fountain model she'd developed last week, utterly disappointed in it, though it wasn't near being complete.

She'd arrived at her usual hour earlier than the rest of her coworkers so she could focus and organize her thoughts. The time she'd spent with Paul on Saturday morning was still fresh in her mind, his request that she return home still tugging at her heartstrings.

But no matter how hard she tried, she couldn't seem to push aside her giddiness—Jack would be back in the office today. Yet Jack was her boss. Her excitement over seeing him again was completely inappropriate, but it remained nonetheless.

A frown slipped into the corner of her mouth. What would Jack think of her fountain? His opinion of her and her creations had become too important to her.

"Knock, knock," Heidi said, leaning into her office. "I hope I'm not disturbing you. You looked engrossed."

Turning away from the computer screen, Rayne looked at Heidi and smiled. "No, you're fine. What are you doing here so early?"

"Had some things to catch up on. I thought better earlier than later. You?"

"Oh, this is my usual time. So, what's up?"

"Nothing, really. Just that several people asked about you at church yesterday. Ever think you'll visit again?"

"I will. I promise." Rayne couldn't think of a reason why she hadn't, at the moment.

"I'm not trying to pry." Heidi's smile brightened. "It's great that you can at least show up at some of the functions. Everyone loves you."

"Thanks for letting me know." Rayne smiled.

"Guess who showed up yesterday."

"I really couldn't say." Rayne edged her gaze back to her computer.

Heidi looked down the hall then leaned forward, talking softly. "Jack. Can you believe it?"

"Huh." Rayne tried to look unfazed, like it wasn't any of her business because, of course, it wasn't. She wasn't going to be like Barb, throwing herself at the man.

"He asked about you."

Jack asked about her? What did Heidi mean, specifically? Did she dare ask for details? Rayne considered what to say next.

Heidi made a face. "I'll catch you later." She disappeared before Rayne could respond.

Jack stepped into her office. "You're here. Good." He shut the door behind him and sat in the chair across from her.

"I see you made it back alive." Rayne chuckled then looked at the model on her computer, hoping to muffle her pounding heart.

"And why wouldn't I?" Jack asked, teasing in his voice.

The sound of it sent tendrils of pleasure up Rayne's spine. She wished she could open a window so the rush of cold air could slap sense into her.

"How did your meeting with the client go? I assume you'll be briefing everyone today."

"Not as well as I had hoped."

His blatant honesty surprised her. Usually people liked to brag about their work, make everything they did sound successful. She faced him and locked her gaze on his eyes. His gorgeous eyes. "What do you mean?"

Jack was the first to break away. Averting his gaze, he looked down and studied his hands. "I took the wrong person with me."

Rayne held her breath. She thought that was a given. "I'm sure you don't mean that. Barb is exceptionally—"

"Talented." Jack cleared his throat. "Yes, I know."

Between the lines, what was Jack saying? Had something happened between them? Rayne wanted to scream, because she couldn't possibly voice these questions. It was none of her business. Yet Jack was in her office, saying much more than he should, she suspected.

"What are you telling me, Jack?"

"I think I could have accomplished more for the client if you had been with me." He glanced at her computer screen, which continued to show the model of the fountain. "You see things differently than others. I'm confident that if you'd visited the site, breathed the air, and viewed the skyline, your creative genius would have kicked in."

Rayne raised her chin in a slow nod. "Ah, now I understand. You've seen my model."

"Yes, I've seen it."

Tension spread through her shoulders. She'd let Jack down.

"My comment has nothing to do with your fountain. I knew I made a mistake about the trip to Dallas before I came in on Saturday morning to see your model." He gave her a soft, reassuring smile.

She relaxed against the chair back, feeling some of her composure return. So Jack still believed in her. "You came in on Saturday just to see it?" The news stunned Rayne. While she was breakfasting with Paul, Jack was looking at her design without her. "I wish I had known."

Jack looked at the clock on the wall. "Listen, Rayne. After being gone for a few days, I've got a lot to catch up on."

With a glance down at her blouse, his eyes lingered, making warmth creep into Rayne's cheeks. She hung on to the breath in her lungs.

"And since you don't have coffee on your shirt today, can you join me for lunch?" He gave her a lopsided grin.

Rayne slowly exhaled. He referred, of course, to her rejecting his invitation before because she'd had to change her blouse. His attempt at humor made her nervous. "I can't think of a single excuse today."

"Good." Jack stood up. "There's a lot we need to discuss."

As Rayne stared up at him, he seemed to be referring to so much more than work. But that was just the imaginings of Rayne's errant and traitorous heart. She took in his determined jaw, rugged good looks, and the emotion in his eyes.

What was he really thinking?

She wanted to run her fingers through his dark hair. Ugh.

He opened her door and took a step into the hall, though one foot remained in her office. "See you later, Rayne."

Then he shut her door, disappearing behind it. When Jack smiled, all was well with the world—except Rayne could not work like this. She knew, beyond any doubt, concern over her relationship with Jack, or lack thereof, had shadowed her fountain. If she continued down this path, FountainTech would suffer along with her reputation.

She'd prayed for an answer, a direction, but God always seemed to be silent when it came to her career path. She doubted attending Heidi's church would give her any more clarity, and she certainly wouldn't attend simply because Jack did.

The headhunter's phone number was saved in her cell phone. She'd find a private moment today to call him and schedule a meeting with him.

A muted knock on the door interrupted her thoughts.

Rayne shook her head. "Come in." What was her office this morning? Grand Central Station?

Barb stuck her head in, a mischievous smile on her face. She slipped through the small opening she'd made and shut the door quietly behind her, then sank into the chair. "Hey, girl."

Elbow on her desk, Rayne put her fingers to her temple. "So, how did it go?" Rayne hadn't wanted to ask, but she knew Barb was expecting her to.

Barb fairly bounced in the chair, though she appeared a little flushed. "You won't believe how well it went."

"Really?" Rayne asked, fearing what she would hear. Barb

had apparently gotten something much different out of the trip to Dallas than Jack had.

❧

One last phone call and Jack would head to Rayne's office and take her to lunch. Maybe out of the office he could dig a little deeper, find out what had been bothering her while she had worked on the design for the fountain model, if anything.

Avoiding her had been a mistake. His entire project could suffer—he wouldn't live up to his reputation, the reason he was hired—if he couldn't control his feelings for Rayne. He would prove to himself today at lunch that he could kill what she stirred in him, that he could work with her and remain oblivious to her charms. He had to. It was his job, and he was a professional.

Jack was back.

He lifted the receiver to return a call when Rayne stepped into his office, looking haggard.

"Jack," she said in a rush of breath, and staggered forward.

"What's wrong?" He sprang from his seat and ushered her into a chair, then closed the door. He kneeled next to her. "Rayne, what's happened?"

She shoved her hands through her hair, pushing it back from her tear-streaked face. "Sorry, just give me a minute. I shouldn't have rushed in here like this."

Jack rose. "Don't tell me. You can't go to lunch."

She stared up at him. "What?"

Seeing the hurt in her eyes killed Jack. "I shouldn't have said that. So, this is serious, isn't it?"

She nodded, sniffling. "It's my father. He's had a heart attack. We think, anyway."

A wall of memories and dark emotions slammed Jack. A house burning with his parents inside. He braced himself against the impact. "I'm so sorry. Is he going to be all right?"

"I don't know. Mom called to tell me. The ambulance is on the way." She peered up at him, a feeble smile slipping onto her lips. "That means I can't have lunch with you."

Jack stuck his hands into his pockets. "Is there anything I can do?"

Rayne nodded. "Forgive me?"

He chuckled, incredulous. "For what?"

"For the fountain. I know it wasn't what you were expecting."

"Rayne, don't worry about that now. Please. Go to your father."

"I might need a few days for this. Just. . . I'll use my vacation time or something."

"I'll take care of it. Don't worry."

She stared out the window as though looking into oblivion, or into the possibility of a morbid future. Funny, Jack only had to look into his past for that.

He held his hand out to her, unsure what he was doing, unsure of her response. She placed her small hand in his, reminding him of the night they'd gone skating and finally held hands, though their gloves were a protective barrier. Her hand was soft and trembling. Using him for support, she stood to her feet.

"Let me walk you to your car," he offered.

She gave him a wary glance. "That's not necessary. I only came to tell you because. . ."

"Because I'm your boss, of course. Plus, we had lunch plans, which you obviously can't keep now. And I'm only walking you to your car because, as a coworker, I want to help."

Her right cheek lifted in a partial smile. "Just so we're clear."

Something wonderful coursed through Jack, despite his continued avoidance of feelings for her. Rayne seemed to be playing the same game that he was playing—dodging an office romance. Her eyes and her words convinced him—but how long could they dance around the obvious?

Jack escorted Rayne to her office, feeling the weight of her crushing news along with her. Coworkers walking the halls could see something was amiss and hung back to watch, questions in their eyes. He would explain everything later. In her office, he assisted her in gathering her briefcase and a few others items, and with his hand on her elbow, he gently guided her through the reception area, out the FountainTech doors, and onto the elevator. He rode down with her.

"Rayne, are you sure you're in a state of mind to drive?"

"They're bringing him to Fargo. It's the nearest hospital with decent cardiology facilities."

"I'll drive you over," Jack said, trying once again to assist her.

The elevator opened, and Jack stepped out with Rayne. She turned to face him and gave a pointed look. "Jack, you don't need to drive me."

Jack didn't get it. Why would she refuse his offer? It stung a little. "If not me, then someone else. What about Heidi?"

"There you are, Rayne." A tall, blond man stepped up to Rayne, jangling car keys.

"Paul," she said, choking back tears.

"Your mom said the ambulance had arrived." Paul wrapped his arm around Rayne's shoulders. "Let's go."

Jack stared, watching the lumberjack-looking guy whisk Rayne away. She appeared to melt into him for support, as though comfortable in his arms. Was this the guy from back home who'd sent the roses? Jack squeezed his fists, scolding himself for probing where he shouldn't. For caring about her in a way that he shouldn't.

Still—Jack clenched his teeth, angry at the determined thoughts—if this man was Rayne's type, how did he even have a chance?

twelve

Sitting in the passenger seat of Paul's truck, Rayne stared at the snow melting against the window as he drove her back to her parents' farm.

After two days of tests, her father had been sent home from the hospital to rest. Though his heart attack was mild in relative terms, lifestyle changes were prescribed. Her father wasn't a man who liked changes. Rayne knew her decisions to go to college and then leave the farming community for the city had been hard on him.

"You okay?" Paul asked.

Rayne tugged her attention from the watery formations on the window to look at him. He watched the road, his glances intermittent and concerned.

"I'm fine." Rayne knew her halfhearted answer was less than convincing. She couldn't help but wonder if she'd caused her father stress because of her unwillingness to comply with his wishes. Yet she was a grown woman.

When would they let her go? Her throat felt like a cardboard box was expanding inside. She'd give herself this ride home to shed the tears, then no more—she had to be strong for her father.

Rayne sucked in a shaky breath then flipped open her cell and called the office. Gail answered in her professional receptionist tone.

"Gail, this is Rayne. Can I speak to Jack?"

"Hi, Rayne. He's in a meeting, but I'm sure he'll want to speak to you."

Rayne feared her connection wouldn't last even though she paid for the best plan in North Dakota.

"Rayne?" Jack came on the line.

"Thanks for talking to me. Gail said you were in a meeting."

"No problem. How's your father?"

"They're sending him home. I need the rest of the week off—maybe even two. I know it's not. . .what others do."

"Everyone is different. Don't beat yourself up."

"I'm willing to use my two-week vacation on this if I have to. It's just that, if I come back to work now, I'll just be a basket case, no good to you."

Jack took a long breath, loud enough for Rayne to hear over the phone. "Just promise me something?"

Rayne glanced over at Paul, who seemed intent on listening, though how could he avoid it? "What's that?"

"When you come back, I want you to put your heart into this project. We'll do everything we can do from this end, but Rayne. . ."

"Yes?"

"I need *you* to make this work. Without you, it won't be the same."

Rayne wasn't certain she liked the burden Jack placed on her; still, there was a part of her that warmed to the fact he had so much faith in her.

"I promise I'll do my best."

"Fair enough."

"Thanks for everything, Jack. I'll call you soon."

Jack was silent for a moment, making Rayne wonder if she'd lost her connection.

"Let me know if there's anything else I can do. And Rayne. . .take care of yourself."

"See you soon." Rayne flipped the phone closed, wondering at the call.

"Your boss seems like a nice guy."

"You could hear him?" She stared at Paul.

"Of course. The cab is pretty quiet, and he was talking loud."

"Yes, he's very nice." Rayne leaned back against the headrest and shut her eyes.

"He seems to think a lot of you."

Rayne let the conversation rest there, refusing to answer.

"What do you think of him?"

Apparently, Paul wasn't willing to let it drop. "I think he's a gifted person and will be good for FountainTech."

"He's seems to be interested in you as more than a coworker."

Rayne jerked her eyes around to Paul, who stared straight ahead at the thickening snow. She hoped they wouldn't run into a whiteout. "How could you know that? You've met twice, once at FountainTech and then again at the hospital."

Rayne thought back to that moment when Jack had come into her father's room to check on his status. The gesture had been a soothing balm to her soul.

"Guys just know. He cares about you."

Rayne sighed then rested her head again. "I'm talking to another company, Paul. I'm not sure I'll be at FountainTech much longer." Rayne wasn't sure why she'd shared the information. She wasn't thinking straight. If she'd thought that telling Paul she wouldn't be working with Jack would ease his concern, it probably didn't make him feel better to know she would be working elsewhere—possibly out of state. Far from her parents' home and from Paul. When Paul didn't say anything else, Rayne let her mind drift back to the crisis with her father. The very second she'd learned of his condition, she feared she might lose him.

In that moment, everything looked different. She would have given anything to have been home and spent time with her parents. She would have given anything for her father to think the absolute best of her. They'd always had a good relationship, and he'd always appeared proud of her. That's why her decision to pursue a profession outside of farm life had been the most difficult decision of her life. Her father hadn't approved. If she came back to stay, would she hear the words of praise from his lips that she longed to hear?

Silently, she prayed. *Lord, help me to know what I should do.*

You know the future. I'm more than willing to do Your will for my life, if only I know what that is.

"We're here," Paul said.

Rayne opened her eyes to watch Paul maneuver his truck around the circular drive in front of the Flemming farmhouse. He jumped from the cab and jogged around to open the door for Rayne. He held his hand out to her.

She took it, feeling the calluses and reassuring strength in his grip, and stepped down.

"I'm here if you need help. Do you hear me? Don't hesitate to call me."

Looking into his eyes, she could see the love behind them. It took her breath away. "Thanks."

She glanced away so he couldn't see her apprehension—fear that he hoped to endear himself to her. But if the small spark she had for him could be kindled. . .

Should she allow that to happen?

Paul tipped her face back to look at him, keeping his hand under her chin. "While you're here, please think about what I said before. You're focused on your father now—I know that. But give us some thought, too, okay?"

Her vision blurred. She pulled herself from his grip, uncertain if she liked his persistence. She trudged up the drive empty-handed because Paul insisted on carrying the luggage. Paul wanted something from her, and for that matter, so did Jack.

Before pushing through the door, she closed her eyes and sucked in a breath, mentally preparing to face whatever might come over the next few days. Jack's handsome face, that brooding look in his eyes, came to mind.

Could Paul be right about Jack caring for her?

❧

Four thirty Friday afternoon, FountainTech offices grew quiet as people left early for the weekend. Jack pulled up the schematics of his invention on his laptop and finished up a few details—a modified pump that he'd labored on for months. He should be ecstatic. And he was, except he hadn't seen Rayne in two weeks. Make that three, because he'd been in Dallas most of the week before her father had his heart attack.

Though she was expected back in the office Monday morning, Jack was beginning to feel uneasy—would she really come back? His team had worked on the fountain in her absence, but her creative touch was the missing ingredient. If Jack could define it, could put a name or label on it, he wouldn't need Rayne—at least for the fountain. . . .

The problem was, Jack should not be feeling this way about the woman—she was off-limits. He'd told himself that a hundred times. But no matter how hard he tried, he hadn't been able to shake her from his thoughts.

Now that he was sure he'd accomplished an engineering feat, was there anyone else he would want to share this news with? Regardless of his feelings, Rayne should be the one to see it first—she would be the person who would see the most potential in it.

Suddenly, Jack couldn't stand it any longer. He flipped open his cell and phoned her.

Getting Rayne's reaction would go a long way in telling him where her thoughts were. If her heart was into coming back to work.

"Hello, Jack?"

Jack closed his eyes, savoring the sound of her voice. *Idiot.* "Hi, Rayne. I hope I didn't interrupt dinner."

She laughed softly. "No, we're just finishing up a card game."

"How's your father?"

"He's much better, though cranky about having to eat low-fat. Bacon and eggs are a staple on the farm, don't you know."

Jack smiled. She sounded good. "And you? How are you holding up?"

"If you're calling to make sure that I'll be at work on Monday, you can count on me to be there."

Monday was three days away. He couldn't wait until then. He really was an idiot. "Actually, Rayne, I have some important news that I need to share with you."

Rayne sucked in a breath. "What is it?"

"Any chance you'll be heading back to Fargo tomorrow?"

Jack heard a man guffawing in the background, and Rayne covered her phone to answer. "I'm sorry, Jack. They were waiting on me. I folded so I could talk to you in private. You're asking if I can come in tomorrow? Has something happened to the fountain?"

Jack hesitated. How did he say this? "Yes and no. I would really rather show you than tell you over the phone."

"And this can't wait? I hadn't planned to come back tomorrow."

Jack cringed and scratched his head as an idea began to form. Could he do that? More importantly, should he?

"I've got it. Why don't I drive out to you? I can show you there." He really was losing it, but the more he thought about it, the more he liked this idea. He wanted to know more about Rayne and her life on a farm. See where she was first inspired to create her designs.

"Are you serious? Jack, I don't think that would be a good idea."

"If I would be intruding, I won't come. But I promise not to take much of your time. Rayne. . .I've been working on this project even before I came to FountainTech." Jack pinched his nose. Should he say it? "I can't think of anyone I would rather share this with than you."

Saying the words left him feeling completely exposed.

"Oh Jack. I didn't mean to sound as though I didn't want you here. That would be rude. I thought you were just making the offer in jest, out of kindness. I would love to see. . ."

"Rayne?"

"I would love to see your project."

Rayne proceeded to give directions, which Jack wrote down.

GPS didn't always work accurately in remote places. He recalled the time when GPS directed him to turn right, only there was a two-hundred-foot drop instead of a road. He didn't need to experience that twice to learn his lesson.

When he hung up, Jack stared at the phone. He wanted to crawl through it to be with her right now. Plus, he allowed himself a grin, a change in scenery would do him good. As he headed home to change clothes before driving to see Rayne, he wondered why he was letting this happen all over again.

Was he destined to destroy his career over women? Then again, he was simply showing her his new design—something that would benefit FountainTech. His initial plan when he first started was to keep his most important asset close to him—that's all he was doing.

On his way out of Fargo, Jack navigated a few slippery spots, heading north toward the Flemming family farm. The nearer he drew to his destination, the more he thought this was a bad idea. He had never been more indecisive.

By seven o'clock that evening, he drove around the circular drive to the farmhouse. As he slowed his vehicle to a stop and turned off the ignition, he watched Rayne talking to Paul next to his big dual-wheeled pickup, the door hanging open. Jack figured the Brawny paper towel man was leaving, but instead of stepping into his truck, he moved away from the door and shut it.

Paul started toward Jack's sports car, Rayne following. She smiled at Jack, a tentative look on her face, and gave him a little wave.

Jack opened his car door and stepped out. This was either a huge mistake or. . .

He was just in time.

thirteen

Jack actually came!

If it weren't for the thrumming in her heart, Rayne would have thought she was seeing things. Apparently, Paul was taken aback as well—he suddenly decided to stay for dinner. Her mother had insisted on having dinner ready for Jack when he arrived, though Rayne explained that Jack would likely eat before he got there.

Paul's long legs carried him too fast, closing the distance between him and Jack. Rayne had to run to pass Paul, making it to Jack first. As she darted in front of Paul, she imagined herself as a barrier between the two, diffusing the tension in the air. Or so she hoped. But she wondered who she was protecting from whom.

She smiled at Jack, oh so glad to see him. "You're just in time for dinner. Have you eaten?"

"Oh, I couldn't intrude like that. I just wanted to get your input on something." He avoided looking at her—*really* looking at her—and glanced at Paul who stood behind her.

Paul thrust out his big hand. "Good to see you again, Jack. If you can't stay, we understand."

Jack shook his hand, a funny look on his face.

Rayne wanted to jab Paul with a stare.

"Dinner's waiting. It would be rude to refuse," she said with a teasing smile, while her heart seemed to stutter at the thought that he might leave so soon.

"Since you put it like that, I'd love to stay," he said, and flashed his dimpled grin.

Then, as if the Jack she knew had suddenly returned, he stared into her eyes, searching.

With Paul standing right behind her—hovering as if he

owned her—the moment was awkward, but in a comical sort of way, like in a funny movie. A blizzard snowing them all in for the weekend would keep things right on track.

Looking down, she dug her foot into the snow and chuckled. "Well, since that's settled, let's go eat."

Rayne struck out toward the farmhouse, confident the two men were close behind.

"What brings you all this way out on a Friday evening?" Paul asked.

"It's regarding a project that Rayne and I are working on. I didn't feel I could wait until she returned." Jack's voice sounded confident, and she sensed that whatever he had created had exhilarated him.

She opened the door, laughing a little inside that neither of the men had thought to open the door for her, proving to the other he was the better gentleman.

"Rayne, can you help me in here?" her mother called from the kitchen.

"You two make yourselves comfortable. Dinner will be ready soon."

Whenever Paul stayed for dinner, which had been a lot lately, he usually helped set the table. This evening he gestured for Jack to join him in the den. Rayne left the two alone and headed toward the kitchen.

After setting the table and putting out the fried chicken, mashed potatoes, and home-grown corn and green beans, Rayne strolled to the den to call the men.

Arms crossed, she hung in the doorway and watched Paul showing Jack one of her father's rifles. "Okay, boys, the fun is over. Let's eat."

Paul snapped the barrel of the rifle shut, and Jack looked up at her, relief spreading over his face.

"I hope you like fried chicken," she said.

Jack's grin was impish, making him look like a little boy. "Love it."

Rayne guided him to the dining room where they usually

ate their evening meal. Her father stood at the head of the table for the first time since his heart attack.

"Dad." She rushed over to him. "You sure you feel up to this?"

Though a little pale, he'd been steadily improving. He squinted an eye at her then looked at Jack and Paul. "Your mother told me I had better come down because you had two suitors here for dinner. Looks like she was right."

Fire spread over her cheeks. She helped her father into his chair. "Jack isn't a suitor, Dad. He's my boss. Do you remember meeting him in the hospital?"

Rayne looked over at Jack. He and Paul remained standing. She assumed they were waiting on her father to be seated. Paul had a triumphant grin on his face. Jack was unreadable.

꣡

Jack sank into the sturdy oak chair at the table across from Rayne, who sat waiting. She smiled at him. She had more color in her face than he'd seen before. He looked down at his empty plate. Being at the farm was good for her.

Paul slid into the seat next to her, only increasing Jack's unease. Eating with the family hadn't been part of his plan. The decision to drive out to the farm had cost him—he'd quickly lost control and now found himself being washed out to sea by a strong current called Rayne. He smiled to himself. With that analogy, Paul was a barracuda.

Suddenly, everyone bowed their heads, and Jack followed suit. Rayne's father said a quick blessing, thanking the Lord for their food and for their guests.

When he finished, Jack slowly lifted his head to the immediate clinking of utensils and dishes being passed around the table. Rayne's father seemed disconnected from the activity as he eyed Jack from the far end of the table.

Rayne's mother dished food onto her husband's plate—a heaping spoonful of mashed potatoes—while he squinted an eye at Jack, studying him.

"The potatoes have got no fat. But you can't have the fried

chicken." She handed him a plate of baked chicken. "Here you go." With a fork, she encouraged a chicken breast onto his place.

"Why'd you make fried chicken, woman? You know it's my favorite."

"For our guests. Rayne said we'd be having company." She looked up from preparing his plate and winked at Jack.

"I didn't say for dinner, Mom." Rayne appeared embarrassed. "But I'm glad you were thinking ahead."

Rayne's father grunted his disapproval, keeping his eyes on Jack. "Rayne tells me you're from Florida."

Jack liked that Rayne had been talking about him. "Yes." But he felt, as had already been suggested, like a suitor on trial. The room tilted a little at the idea.

Paul passed the mashed potatoes to Jack. "What part?"

"The sunny part." Jack dropped a large spoonful of the potatoes on his plate and laughed at his own joke, then looked up to a table of stares.

Rayne was the only other person who chuckled. "I'm sure it's hard for Jack, coming from a warmer state to North Dakota."

As soon as Jack finished eating, he'd have to find a way to show Rayne the reason he came then escape. Fortunately, the rest of dinner wasn't focused too much on him. Paul and Rayne's father hogged the conversation, engrossed in a farm-related discussion.

Make that weather-related.

Corn, soybeans, wheat, winter wheat, dry beans, barley, durum, potatoes, sugar beets, sunflowers, canola, oats. Then there was the soil temperature, and was it too wet or too dry? And the weather—was it too hot, too cold, or too windy? Would it be early planting or late planting this year? The worst cases, of course, were the extremes of flooding or drought.

Fascinated by it all, Jack smiled to himself. Both men were thoughtful and intelligent. Jack quickly recognized how important farming was to them—it was their whole life, consuming most of their time and obviously their thoughts.

If he were in their position, how could he blame them? Now that he considered it, most of his thoughts and time were consumed with his career, his evenings spent on related engineering projects.

"They say we can expect a drought this year." Paul slid his plate forward a half inch and leaned against the chair back.

"Don't remind me. Say, did you hear that Tom Bly broke his leg?"

"Yep, that's too bad."

"As soon as I'm feeling myself again, I need to get up the road and pay him a visit."

"That'll be soon enough, Gary." Rayne's mother rose to gather up the dishes.

Rayne stood, too. "I'll do the dishes, Mom, since you did most of the cooking."

"Nonsense. You've got guests."

"I'll help her, Mrs. Flemming," Paul said, throwing a quick glance at Jack.

Of all the. . .

Apparently, Paul was attempting to earn points. Jack wasn't sure he was entered in the contest for Rayne, even if he wanted to be.

When Rayne leaned over him to take his plate, she smiled down. "We usually wait for an hour after dinner for dessert. Would you like yours now?"

"No, thank you, on dessert. I need to get back."

"Just give me a few minutes to finish the dishes. Then you can show me the reason for your trip."

Paul hung around the table, grabbing up the remaining utensils. Jack stood. He could do something at least. He picked up the larger platters that held the remaining food.

Rayne's father rose from his place at the table. "It was good to see you again, Jack."

Jack paused, holding a plate with two pieces of fried chicken left. "I'm glad you're doing better."

"Not at the moment. I need to lay down now." He walked

slowly from the dining room, Rayne's mother hovering near his elbow, then turned back. "Take good care of my little girl at that company of yours if you want to keep her."

"Of course I will, sir." Jack nodded with an easy smile.

"Just remember, we could use her here, too."

With that, Rayne's father began climbing the stairs. Her father had just confirmed Jack's fears—making Jack glad he'd come for the first time since he'd arrived. He finished helping clear the table, but with Paul lingering near Rayne in the kitchen, and her mother, having returned from helping Mr. Flemming, chattering away, it was too crowded for Jack.

He made his way to the den to wait for Rayne. He'd been there less than two minutes when she appeared and grabbed his arm. "Come on." She looked back through the wide doorway. "Hurry."

Jack stood. "Where are we going?"

"Shh." She crept through the front door, and Jack gently closed it behind them. "Follow me."

Jack hurried behind her through the snow. It was beginning to come down hard and thick, and the chill seeped through his sweater. "Rayne, what are you doing?"

"Hiding." Rayne trotted ahead to the barn about forty yards from the house. She tugged Jack inside.

"What's going on? Why are we in the barn?" Jack rubbed his shoulders. "Shouldn't we have at least put on our coats?"

Rayne giggled. "I don't think Paul is ever going to leave as long as you're here. This was the only way for us to speak privately."

Couldn't she just ask Paul to leave? Jack looked at her, noticing that the dim light in the barn created a halo around Rayne's face. Her expression, her features, appeared soft and. . .beautiful.

"Now, what was so important that you drove out here?" She folded her arms, teasing in her eyes.

She had beautiful eyes, too. They were deep and penetrating tonight.

Suddenly, Jack's mind went completely blank. Why had he come to the farm? He shook his head, searching for the words. The pump. . .

"I designed a new fountain pump. It's more efficient, using less horsepower and yet streaming higher than any other."

Her eyes brightened. "Are you kidding me? I'm thrilled for you, Jack."

Jack sagged, uncertain if he witnessed all the enthusiasm in her eyes he'd hoped for. He was an idiot. "The schematic is in my car."

She took a step toward him. "You drove all this way to show it to me?"

"I. . .uh. . .well, yes." The huge barn felt like it was closing in on him. He stared at the ground and tugged at his shirt collar sticking out of his sweater, then looked back at Rayne. "I'm sorry. I just thought you would understand."

"I do understand. I'm already thinking of a fountain design. I'm just flattered that you wanted to share it with me."

"Who else?" The cold, the smell of the barn, the pump design, all disappeared from his world because his focus was now on Rayne's face alone. When had she come so near to him?

She tipped her head just so, the way she'd done the night they'd gone ice-skating. He'd wanted to kiss her then but hadn't. He'd thought about kissing her ever since that moment.

Jack relinquished the last of his control and gave in to his natural impulse, leaning toward Rayne, meeting her. At that moment, she was all that mattered to him.

He pressed his lips against her perfectly shaped ones and melted into their softness.

&

Delight spread over Rayne, rippling from the top of her head, then down her body, all the way to her toes. Contentment enveloped her, and yet she wanted more. . . .

So much more.

As if in answer to her heart's longing, Jack wrapped his

arms around her, drawing her closer. Of their own accord, her arms slid up and over his shoulders then around his neck. She weaved her fingers through his hair, his wonderful hair. How she'd longed to do just that.

She melted into him, balancing between the dizzy heat of his kiss and the reality of the cold barn enclosing them. With all her heart, she wanted his kiss to intensify, but a noise tugged her back from the edge, the world around her entering into her awareness.

Gently, she unwrapped herself from this man who'd captivated her heart. "Oh Jack," she whispered, pressing her head against his broad chest. There she felt content, safe. Like she belonged.

She breathed in the scent of his cologne, making her lightheaded. Finally, she eased away from him and gazed into his eyes, a dreamy, faraway look in them.

She adored the lazy grin on his face.

Someone cleared his throat. Rayne stiffened. Paul stepped from the shadows.

At seeing him, her heart raced. She dreaded reading his expression. Had he witnessed the kiss she'd shared with Jack? Their tender moment?

"Sorry to interrupt your discussion," he said, tension twisting his voice.

"No problem." Rayne and Jack answered simultaneously, both appearing eager to hide their indiscretion.

Rayne grimaced. Indiscretion? Had she been reckless in kissing Jack?

Appearing hesitant, Paul looked from Jack to Rayne, an awkward silence filling the barn.

"Your mother was looking for you," he finally said.

"I need to head home anyway." Jack jammed his hands into his pocket and blew out a breath. He gave a nervous chuckle. "Besides, it's getting late."

Jack headed for the barn door, as did Rayne. She gave Paul a soft smile in an attempt to hide her annoyance as well as reassure him, though she wasn't sure why. She didn't owe Paul an explanation. Did she?

Outside, Rayne wrapped her arms around herself as the threesome hurried to the farmhouse. The weather had taken a turn for the worse. Once inside, Rayne stomped her shoes on the rug.

Jack did the same then reached for his coat on the coat rack. "Thanks for dinner, Rayne. I hope I wasn't too much trouble tonight." He subtly glanced at Paul, who remained in the foyer with them.

Paul thrust his hand out to Jack. "It was good to see you, Jack."

Ready to explode, Rayne pursed her lips instead.

"And where do you think you're going, mister?" Rayne's mother appeared in the foyer, hands on hips.

Before Jack could answer, her mother closed the distance between them and tugged on his coat. "You can't go out in this weather. There's a serious storm brewing out there."

"I don't remember hearing anything about a storm."

"Wasn't supposed to be here until Sunday. We've got plenty of room, and another day at the farm won't kill you. But driving a lone North Dakota road as far as you have to go just might."

Rayne stared at the floor, laughing inside. This was one time she more than appreciated her mother's gift for persuasion.

•

fourteen

Yawning, Rayne rubbed her eyes. She felt oddly at peace with the world.

Happy. She knew there was some reason for this feeling inside. But what was it? Still groggy, she searched her thoughts.

Then she remembered. Jack was here at the farm.

And in the barn last night. . .

She shut her eyes and allowed her mind to linger on Jack's kiss. With her finger, she traced her mouth, recalling his lips against hers, and drew in a long breath.

Suddenly, Paul's kiss came to mind. Though at the time, she had felt the tiniest rekindling of any feelings she might have harbored for Paul, his kiss had not stirred things in her like Jack's—his kiss potent, making her heady with emotions she'd never experienced before.

She allowed the rush of excitement to swirl once again.

A big smile spread across her face. She'd have to tone that down, she knew. It wouldn't do to have people asking questions. How would she explain?

Filling her room was a calm that she easily recognized as the muted quiet of a snow-covered landscape. The blue and yellow wallpaper reflected a shimmer from a break in the curtains hanging against the window. A white radiance only created by snow. Or did everything just look brighter today?

A million questions bombarded her thoughts—what did this mean? Did Jack feel the same way she did this morning? How would they work together now?

With a single kiss, her relationship with Jack had altered into something much more than coworkers. Something much more than friends. Oh how this changed everything.

But for better or worse? Rayne wasn't sure she wanted to know.

And what would he think if she told him she had been talking to another company?

On the side table, her cell chirped, letting her know she had a text message. She reached over and lifted the phone.

From Jack. He'd left the text message in the middle of the night? She'd slept hard, then, because she hadn't heard the message come through.

Rayne rose up on her elbows to read the words, *Forgive for my actions. Leaving first thing in the morning.*

What? Pain stabbed her heart. Was he sorry for kissing her? Or was he afraid of Rayne's reaction? What might have happened, what might he have said, had Paul not interrupted them in the barn?

Though her mother had convinced Jack to stay the night to be safe, they'd not had another moment alone. And now it didn't look like she'd get one.

Rayne wasn't so sure it would be safe for him to drive back this morning either. Worry for his safety tore through her. Apprehension over his apparent regret of kissing her sank heavily in the pit of her stomach.

Rayne rose from bed and thrust open the curtains. It was snowing so hard she couldn't see the barn from her window. She pulled on her jeans and a sweatshirt and opened the door. The aroma of bacon and eggs met her as she bounced down the stairs, hoping.

When Rayne turned the corner into the kitchen, her heart leaped.

Jack sat at the kitchen table, her mother's best breakfast spread before him. He was buttering toast and, though he smiled, uncertainty lingered in his eyes.

She couldn't help the big smile she launched at him.

Her father busied himself, scooping fat-free margarine from a tub, frowning. Her mother turned from the hefty pan of bacon she was frying and glanced at Rayne. "Good morning, sugar pie."

Rayne hoped her father wasn't eating the bacon. "Good morning." She tugged out a chair and sat at the table, tossing a questioning look at Jack. "You're not going to drive in this, are you?"

Her mother leaned over the table, setting a plate of eggs in the middle. "Of course not. He's agreed to stay for at least another day." Her mother winked. "Isn't that right, Jack?"

His dimples deepened with his smile, along with the color in his face. "Looks like a blizzard out there."

Rayne hung her head, allowing a soft laugh. Her mother appeared to have a way with Jack. A way that she didn't have with Rayne ever since she'd taken the job in Fargo.

Rayne's father chuckled. He looked like the image of vigor this morning. Jack was good for him. Apparently, he was good for them all.

Had they given up on Paul, then? At the thought, Rayne was surprised he hadn't made his way over this morning, especially after walking in on her and Jack in the barn. He'd been right about Jack caring about her. She saw that now. Would Paul continue to pursue her, or would he step out of the picture?

Rayne grabbed a slice of bacon and crunched on it while her mother poured her a glass of orange juice. Jack and her father discussed weather. Good. Jack was fitting in.

Rayne focused on eating breakfast and pondered what this day would bring, snowed in with her family and a man she couldn't stop thinking about.

&

Jack smiled for Rayne's family, but he was suffocating inside, feeling like a first-class moron. He'd wanted—no, needed—to see her. He'd needed to show her his design, so he'd driven to her family's farm. Who does something like that?

A moron, that's who. A moron on the fast track to losing his focus and, worse, his job, if he kept this up.

And then what did he go and do? He'd kissed her. Listening to her father tell him an account in which he'd almost lost the farm that had been in the family for years, Jack nodded but was only half listening as he glanced over at Rayne. He looked down at his plate, shuffled his eggs around, and daydreamed about kissing her again.

Rayne possessed something that Jack found irresistible. He couldn't have imagined something so powerful could emanate from her. She seemed like such a quiet, creative soul. But maybe that's where the secret lay, and he was drawn to her in a way that he was never drawn to Kiera, Rayne's exact opposite.

Jack took a bite of the eggs. This was all so. . .unexpected. It wasn't part of his plan.

"Never, ever take your eyes of the mark, off the goal," her father said, and continued with his farm tale.

The words seemed to stab at Jack's heart, at his mistake this weekend. He'd prided himself in being a focused man, shooting for the goal. But now his focus was a jumbled mess.

Rayne's father had a penchant for tossing out proverbial words of wisdom. Most were true and well placed, of course, but over time a person might think he sounded a bit condescending. Still, Jack liked him. He was a good man. And clearly, Rayne loved her father, her family, deeply.

He sensed she struggled with being away from them.

"Well, I'm going to rest. Thank you for breakfast, Mamma." Rayne's father scooted from the table and took his plate to the sink where Mrs. Flemming was already doing the dishes. He leaned over and kissed her on the cheek.

Jack felt a little guilty for catching them in a personal moment. Rayne was lucky to have her parents, a family to go home to for a visit. Something Jack had lost long ago. Memories Jack had worked hard to shove from his mind began to seep back in. What was he going to do all day to keep his mind from them?

Rayne's father shuffled from the kitchen, Rayne at his side.

Jack stood and moved next to her mother at the sink.

"Is there something I can do?" he asked. "Since I'm here until the storm lets up a little, maybe I can help."

She stuck a dish into the dishwasher and chuckled. "Well, when Paul finishes up at his own place, he's heading over here. As soon as the weather lets up a bit"—she peered out the kitchen window at the clouds—"and it looks like that'll be soon, maybe you can help break the ice on the ponds for the cattle."

"Uh, sure, I can do that." He didn't have a clue how. "As long as you don't think I would be more of a hindrance to Paul than a help."

A warm hand slid over his shoulder. Rayne was at his side. "I'll help. Jack isn't accustomed to farmwork, Mom."

Jack bristled but then saw the teasing in Rayne's eyes. What was he getting into? "I can work."

"Are you sure about that?" Rayne squeezed his bicep and smiled, color creeping into her cheeks.

Good thing he worked out.

Rayne's mother laughed. "I know what you're thinking. The snow is too deep for the truck, even if it's a four-wheel drive."

"That's what I'm thinking, all right." Rayne smiled, a twinkle in her eyes.

Her mother thrust her hands into the steaming dishwater, apparently washing the dishes before sticking them in the dishwasher. "A few years ago, Rayne talked her daddy into using snowmobiles to feed the cattle during the winter. She could talk her daddy into just about anything."

Rayne had turned a farm chore into something she considered fun. He smiled down at her. Right there, in the kitchen, with her mother standing next to them, Jack wanted to kiss her again. He looked at the smile on her soft lips, recalling how it had felt to kiss her, how his soul had stirred. His gaze traveled back up to her eyes.

Had she been thinking of that as well?

"Before you head out, can you stoke the fire for me?" her mother asked.

"I'll show Jack what to do and then be back to help you finish up here."

Jack followed Rayne out the kitchen door to the back porch where she loaded his arms with logs for the fire. In the distance, Jack spotted a familiar truck lumbering down the road.

Rayne carried a few logs as well, and Jack followed her into the living room where they stacked the wood against the wall a short distance from the large wood-burning stove.

"Mom and Dad use this to help heat the house." She stood straight and gestured to the stove. "Just stick a few logs in while I go help Mom finish up in the kitchen. Then we'll head out."

Jack snickered. He had the feeling Rayne was enjoying bossing him around for a change. Peering inside the stove, he carefully placed a couple of logs inside. Boots stomped near the front door; then it swung open.

Jack turned to see Paul standing in the small foyer, tugging off his gloves and glancing around the house. "Anyone home? I came to help with the chores."

His gaze landed on Jack, and Paul frowned.

fifteen

Sitting on her snowmobile, Rayne looked up at the sky and saw a small break in the clouds as the heavier snow moved to the east of them. She watched Jack shove the last of the hay from the small trailer attached to the snowmobile. Fortunately, they didn't keep many cattle, or using the snowmobiles would have taken them too long.

She smiled to herself, thinking about the day she'd talked her father into them. She'd wanted a snowmobile for fun, of course, but on a farm, pretty much every purchase has to be work-related. Of course, her father didn't use them, preferring the truck, and Rayne had been gone the last few years at school and then to work.

For the first time, she considered that her father might have purchased the snowmobiles as a way to keep her on the farm, entice her to stay. Regret seeped into her thoughts.

"Hey, what's wrong?" Jack stomped over to her.

Had she allowed her momentary doubts to show? She took stock of Jack, who wore her father's too-big extra work boots, farm clothes, and coat. She liked the look on him. "You know, you make a better farmer than I thought you would."

Jack fired off his big-dimpled grin again. It warmed her cold bones all the way to the marrow.

"You're enjoying this, aren't you?" He kept smiling as he waited for her answer.

She couldn't help the laugh that escaped. "Yes."

He closed the distance between them and snatched the cap from her head. Laughing, she didn't have the strength to grab it back as they wrestled.

Rayne shoved Jack a little too hard, and he toppled, pulling her with him. The snow hit her face, sobering her, and she looked at Jack's face, so near hers. "Are you up for a little fun?" She pushed to her feet and dusted off the remaining snow.

Still on the ground, Jack studied her, taking his time to answer. "Sure."

"Let's unhitch these trailers then. We can grab them on the way back."

After freeing the snowmobiles from the trailers, she hopped on and sped away, listening for Jack to do the same. Quickly enough, she heard the whir of his snowmobile behind her.

The sky was beginning to clear, turning the day beautiful. Rayne enjoyed the freedom of speeding across the snow, and the wind, though cold, gusting against her cheeks, and best of all, Jack enjoying the day with her. Snowmobiling was one of her favorite things. What could be better than doing this with someone she. . . What exactly did she feel for Jack?

Rayne shoved the serious thoughts to the back of her mind so she could enjoy this moment. It might never come again. She sped up and glanced back. Jack wasn't far behind, and his snowmobile jerked forward as he squeezed the throttle, giving it more gas.

His bright smile flashed, and Rayne turned her back to him, intending to race far ahead. Laughing, she whirred over a rift and felt the jar, even though she'd plummeted into soft snow. The family farm was a little over a thousand acres. Soon she'd reach the place she wanted to show Jack.

As she drew near the copse of trees, Rayne slowed the snowmobile to a stop. Jack joined her, grinning from ear to ear.

She tugged off her helmet. "So, what did you think?"

"I think there's more to farming than meets the eye."

Rayne laughed and slid from the recreational vehicle's seat. "We won't hear the end of this, just so you know. Work before play."

"Are you saying we weren't finished with the chores?" Jack

hopped off his snowmobile.

"Are you kidding?" Rayne began trudging toward the trees and motioned for Jack to follow. "Come on."

Rayne made her way through the trees, stepping in thick snow. Soon her breathing was becoming harder.

Jack sidled next to her. "Where are you taking me?"

"You'll see. Say, why aren't you breathing hard? You can't be in that great of shape."

"This isn't exactly exerting to me. But I admit, the morning chores made me a little tired." He grinned.

As Rayne neared the edge of the grove that opened up to a small bluff, she snuck another peek at Jack. This was her secret place, yet she'd brought him here.

When they broke through the trees, Rayne stopped. "This is it. It's not much, but this bluff gives me a good view of the surrounding area."

"It's beautiful, Rayne."

"I come here to think and pray." Why was she sharing this with him? She angled her head at him to gauge his reaction.

"Is this where you came to watch the fields, where you were inspired to create your designs?"

Rayne huffed a laugh. He'd brought the fact that they work together back into the mix. Funny how she'd tried to forget that part of their relationship.

"Rayne, I'm sorry if I offended you last night. . . . I shouldn't have—"

"Oh Jack. I wasn't offended. I kissed you back. Couldn't you tell?" Despite her willing them away, tears welled in her eyes.

She turned to face him, and suddenly he was there, sweeping her up in his arms yet again. His lips pressed hard against hers this time, and she slid her arms over his chest, her hands around his neck, drawing him downward, closer.

❧

Rayne was in his arms. What more could he want? He savored the moment, feeling her small form against his, her tender lips responding to his. . . .

No, no, no, man. What are you doing? Jack gently untangled himself from Rayne, and with both hands, held her at arm's length. "Rayne. . ."

Rayne frowned, and tears flooded her eyes. "Jack?"

"What are we doing?" He released her and, shaking his head, turned his back on her to stare out over the snow-covered landscape. "I'm an idiot."

"What are you trying to say, Jack?"

What happened to the guard he'd erected around his heart? He shoved a hand through his hair. "I should never have come to the farm to see you."

Jack could hear the strain in Rayne's responding sigh.

"I admit, I find you irresistible. That makes me vulnerable, and I can't work like this. We can't work like this."

"What if. . .what if I work somewhere else?"

Incredulous, Jack chuckled and stared down at the ground. Suddenly the cold was beginning to creep through all the layers he wore. "Not a good idea either. You see, FountainTech won't work without you. I can't make it the premier water feature design company. You're the key. . ." *To my heart.*

Jack shrugged off the errant thought. Getting romantically involved with Rayne hadn't been part of his plan.

When she didn't answer, Jack realized how that must have sounded. Like he was putting the company before any feelings he had for her. His shoulders tensed. Wasn't that exactly what he was doing? But his reasons involved so much more than the company.

"Rayne, please accept my apology."

She was staring at her feet. He lifted her chin and slid his thumb down her cheek. "I care for you. I think you know that."

"Why? Because you come out to my farm, stay with my family, kiss me, and now. . ."

"That's exactly why I'm putting a stop to my actions now. I never should have come here. I made a mistake."

"Well, that's just great, Jack. Thank you for sharing." Rayne began stomping back through the trees.

Jack followed, feeling as if he'd made a monumental blunder. But he wasn't sure which mistake was worse—coming to the farm and allowing the kiss with Rayne or now rejecting her.

What a jerk he was.

He trudged behind her, hoping to make her understand. "You should know I'm damaged goods. I'm no good for you as anything other than your boss."

"I'm not sure you'll have to worry about that much longer."

Jack hoped Rayne didn't mean that. "What? You're not going to quit, are you? Look, I apologized, didn't I?"

"You said it yourself—we can't work together."

Jack snatched her around to face him.

Seeing her so visibly shaken pierced his heart to the core. How could he hurt her like this? "All right."

She frowned, confused. "All right, what?"

Jack gently tugged her toward him. She resisted at first then willingly came into his arms. He pressed his face into the crook of her neck. "Let's try to make this work. I can't stand to hurt you."

She drew away from him. "So you want to try this, whatever it is between us, because you feel sorry for me?"

"No, that's not what I mean. I feel sorry for myself. I would be a mess without you. But we have to be careful. We have to take this slow. It wouldn't do for anyone at work to know. Not yet. We need to keep this personal and private."

"I think Barb is the only one who would care."

"Don't kid yourself. There are plenty who are jealous of you. They would think I'm showing you favoritism. Harold would certainly care."

"You're right, then. We should take this much slower." Rayne reached for the handlebars of the snowmobile, preparing to throw her leg over.

This weekend Jack had seen a different side to Rayne. He'd

watched her maneuver a snowmobile like a pro, watched her break ice on a pond and feed cattle, watched her interact with her family.

Grief squeezed his chest. "You know, seeing you with your family reminds me of. . ."

Emotions lodged in his throat, creating an ache.

Rayne released the handlebars and slid her hand over his shoulder to rest on his arm. "Of what?"

"My own family. They're gone now though."

"What happened?"

"They died in a fire."

"Oh Jack," she whispered, her eyes watering. "I'm so sorry."

"Reminds me of all I've lost." He'd closed this off for years, kept it buried, and now he wasn't sure he wanted to experience the pain again.

She stared up at him, more than concern emanating from her face.

At the moment, Rayne was all Jack wanted. But why did caring for her have to be so complicated? Why did being with her invoke painful memories?

Growing close to Rayne would cost him.

sixteen

Jack ballooned his cheeks, capturing air in his mouth before releasing it in a sigh. Staring at his computer screen, he saw nothing but the mess he'd made of everything. When he'd first accepted the position with FountainTech and moved to North Dakota, he'd had big plans for himself and for the company.

First, he'd planned on getting his personal life back on track. Kiera was out of his life for good. He wouldn't have to see her every day at work, or happen upon her anywhere in the state of California. Second, he wanted a new start professionally—this time *he* was heading up a division and calling the shots.

Jack's desk phone rang, but he was too busy looking at everything that had not been accomplished in the last few weeks. Nothing appeared to be going as planned or on schedule. And the fountain design itself—Rayne had not been involved in the process enough to touch it with her magic. Granted, she'd taken time to be with her father as he recovered.

This week she was back in the office, focusing on tweaking the fountain design the rest of his team had labored on in her absence. Passing her office to get his morning coffee, Jack couldn't decide whether to stop and say hello. They'd agreed to slow down their rapidly accelerating relationship. Fortunately, someone had been in Rayne's office, effectively making the decision for him.

Once in his own office again, Jack leaned back in his chair and clasped his hands behind his head. He almost regretted that he'd been right about how much he needed her to make his plans for FountainTech work. Depending that much on one person was never a good idea.

He thought about how that wisdom applied to matters of the heart as well. How had he become this attached to Rayne so quickly? Though his painful and embarrassing breakup with Kiera two days before their wedding had happened months ago, that wasn't enough time, was it?

The phone rang again. Jack ignored it. Calls always came through the receptionist unless he'd given out his direct number, which he hadn't. *Take a message, Gail.*

So much for his "Jack is back" motto. His vow to avoid love had crumbled the second he'd looked into the deep pool of Rayne's eyes. They'd brimmed with emotion, seemingly giving a meaning to his life he didn't realize he needed.

And then going to the farm had dragged out memories he'd kept buried for years. They'd tortured him since leaving Rayne's farm two days ago. But now that he was back in the real world, he saw things clearly—caring for her the way he did wasn't good for either of them, and apparently it wasn't good for FountainTech either.

He was off his game.

A soft knock on the door jolted him back to his surroundings. "Come in."

Gail stuck her head in. "Uh, Jack. I've been trying to reach you."

He leaned forward to lift a pen on his desk and shuffle through a stack of paperwork. "I know. I'm busy. Didn't you take a message or send it to voice mail?"

She frowned. "Harold wants you in his office five minutes ago."

Jack stilled. "I'm on my way."

He snatched up his laptop, dreading Harold's untimely request. Had he heard something about Jack and Rayne? Pasting a confident smile on his face, he strode down the hall to Harold's office. If he smiled big enough, he just might convince himself that he was on top of things before he got there.

With the back of his knuckles, he gave a knock on the opened door and grinned. "You wanted to see me?"

Frowning, Harold focused on the papers strewn over his desk. "Come in and shut the door," he said without looking up at Jack.

Not good. Jack did as he was told and tried to ignore the shrinking feeling he always had around Harold. But that was the man's intention—he loved to intimidate.

While Jack waited for Harold to acknowledge him, he opened his laptop. Harold wasn't the only one who was busy. Jack could give as good as he got.

Harold cleared his throat. Jack pulled his gaze from the laptop screen and shut it, smiling.

"How's the creative design team doing?" Harold rocked back in his leather executive chair.

Jack guessed that Harold had heard something, or else he wouldn't be asking the question in this manner. They had meetings for this sort of thing, where Jack would present a PowerPoint that he'd prepared ahead of time.

Maintaining his confident veneer, Jack tugged his laptop open and waited for the screen to load the image of the water sculpture the team had been working on. He placed the laptop on the desk, allowing Harold to see, and smiled like he was a proud new father. Harold might not notice anything missing.

As Jack expected, Harold simply nodded, unaffected by what would normally mesmerize anyone else.

"The client wants to move the project up by two months," Harold said.

Jack stared. *Two months?* And he was already behind.

"Don't let me down, champ. I'm counting on you."

How could Harold have agreed to that? It was lunacy. At the moment, Jack was too stunned to think of an adequate response, but he had to recover, give Harold something— anything—so he could remain his "champ," even though he hated the reference.

"I've got something you should see," Jack said. Sooner or later he planned to share the news with Harold anyway, though before he did that, he'd prefer to be certain it would perform the way he hoped.

"What's that?"

On his computer, Jack pulled up the schematics for his new pump.

Harold leaned forward, appearing a little curious, momentarily taken aback.

Good. Jack had made the right decision. His confidence began to soar for real now.

Harold put on his black-framed reading glasses to study the schematic more closely. "Anyone else know about this?"

⋙

Rayne rubbed her eyes then squinted at the design team as she explained again the nuances that she'd added to the fountain—what Jack had defined as Rayne's magic. She hoped he was right, because she was certainly not feeling the magic today.

Instead, she was beginning to feel the sleep deprivation of the last couple of weeks as the team had labored hard to make the new deadline. Add to that, they were in the middle of a bid for another large-scale water sculpture and would need to start on that one immediately. All of the busyness had trumped any expectations she had of having time with Jack.

She caught a glimpse of him in her peripheral vision, leaning against the back wall as though standing out of her way. His lean physique distracted her. As the team members, including Simon and Barb, discussed the fountain, Rayne couldn't focus on their words. The kisses she had shared with Jack seemed like a lifetime ago. The pressure they had been under to complete this fountain was probably a good thing—keeping them both busy. Keeping her from having time to think about Jack. Or his kiss.

Still, she felt that something between them had changed. Yes, she and Jack had decided to slow things down, but she sensed a distancing in him. And she'd noticed he'd been purposefully avoiding her—his creative lead.

The way things were working out, Rayne was almost thankful that her mind had been consumed with work. Even though the team's ramped-up schedule had forced her to reschedule her lunch interview to this evening.

Oh Jack, I hope you understand. . . . She drew in a ragged breath, hoping that entertaining thoughts of a new opportunity at another company wasn't a mistake. Working somewhere else could give her and Jack freedom to explore whatever was between them. Maybe even give her a chance for the promotion she'd lost at FountainTech.

Except there was one small detail that needed to be worked out. The man she would be interviewing with tonight, Carvis Clark, had lured her with the possibility she could work from Fargo and not have to leave North Dakota. That incentive persuaded her to at least listen to him.

Suddenly, she realized that everyone was staring at her. "I. . .uh, I'm sorry. Did I miss something?"

"I'm still not seeing it, Rayne." Simon smirked. "What exactly makes this fountain better than what we did before you worked your *magic*?"

Rayne frowned, never having heard Simon speak to her this way. Jack was right—Simon was jealous.

"All right, let's break for lunch." Jack stepped into the fray, standing next to the computer screen. "You've all been working very hard to meet the new deadline. I'm proud of you. We'll meet again tomorrow—plan for a working lunch."

A few sighs and groans escaped the group, and Jack frowned. Rayne knew they all probably blamed him for accepting the new deadline. She grabbed her notepad to leave, a small part of her wishing that Jack would tug on her sleeve, ask her to stay behind while he discussed some attribute of the fountain he wanted added.

That would have been a normal thing to do. It would even have been expected. Instead, as she swung open the door, she glanced behind her to see Barb sliding herself to sit exotically on the conference table.

"Jack? I've got some ideas I'd like to share with you." She crossed her slender legs, easily showing them off with the short skirt she wore.

For a moment, Rayne hung back, waiting—no, hoping—that Jack would shove Barb away, or at least flash Rayne an apologetic I'm-sorry-I-have-to-endure-this look. But no, he simply smiled at Barb.

Burning with rage, Rayne shoved the rest of the way through the door and marched down the hall to her office, the surroundings a blur. She slammed her office door behind her, quickly regretting it. Someone would certainly question her actions, and then what was she supposed to say? That she didn't appreciate Jack smiling at Barb, responding to her flirtation?

Rayne covered her face with her hands, hating the tears that came. *Lord, I can't do this. I can't keep this up.*

❧

Jack smiled down at Barb, careful to keep his gaze on her face and not on the bait she dangled.

"It's difficult to find time to talk to you with this new schedule. How about dinner tonight? I could share some of my ideas then, away from the pressure of the office." She toyed with the solitaire diamond hanging against the bare skin at the edge of her low-cut blouse just above. . .

Jack jerked his gaze back up to her eyes. In them he witnessed a look of victory, as though she'd seen his eyes traveling where they ought not to go. "I'm sorry, Barb, but I have a project that I'm working on at home, too, and I have to complete that soon. Maybe you could come in, say, about seven in the morning. We could meet before things heat up around here."

Inside, he cringed at his word choice. He suspected Barb wanted things to heat up.

She smiled, a slight quiver on her shiny, glossed lips.

"Seven it is. Before things heat up." She slid from the conference table, and Jack couldn't help himself; he watched as her willowy legs carried her to the conference room door. She tugged the door open with a slight twist and sassy glance back in his direction, catching his look once again.

Jack flamed inside, angry that any woman would use her attributes like that. He raged that he'd been watching her without even realizing it, before he could stop himself.

He had no feelings toward her whatsoever, not even lust. Rubbing his temples, he closed his eyes. He had so much work to do in addition to completing his pump. He wanted to test that soon. But all he could think about was Rayne. She must be terribly hurt.

Maybe. . .could that be for the best?

seventeen

"My contract included a noncompete clause. What about that?" Rayne toyed with the chicken breast on her plate and glanced up at Mr. Clark. She refused to eat the broccoli that came with her dish for fear it would end up in her teeth.

In his midthirties, Carvis Clark wore expensive-looking tan slacks and a cream-colored polo shirt with a tweed sports jacket. He looked—and she hated herself for this— very good. Since when did she make a habit of noticing handsome men?

Since. . .Jack? Rayne hated the fact that Jack was so handsome, because she wasn't the only one who'd noticed him. An image of Barb sitting on the conference table, crossing her legs in a short skirt, while Jack stood there, burned in her thoughts. Bile seared the back of her throat.

Mr. Clark cleared his throat, tugging her focus back to the interview. She took a sip of water, hoping it would hide the heat she felt in her face.

He'd invited her to meet him at Giovanni's, a pricey Italian restaurant in West Fargo. Initially, he'd wanted to fly her out to Southern California for the interview, but with FountainTech's schedule, and the fact that Rayne had recently taken off to be with her father, she couldn't afford the time to get away. So, here she was, sitting across from Mr. Carvis Clark, vice president of Elemental Innovations, Inc.

He flashed his perfect, white smile—the guy was as slick as they came, Rayne thought.

"California doesn't recognize noncompete clauses, even one signed in another state, and regardless, you might find that yours has expired by now. And if it makes you feel better, we've made plans to move into some new market niches, which I can't share with you just yet, but we've no plans to compete with FountainTech directly."

Rayne offered a flat smile. He had a point there. She'd worried needlessly, and yet she'd agreed to meet him in spite of her concerns.

Mr. Clark laid his silverware on the side of his plate and his napkin on the table, indicating he'd finished.

Rayne was relieved and hoped he wouldn't expect her to stay for dessert. She'd barely touched the food on her plate as it was. She glanced at her watch. Nine thirty already?

"It's getting late. I should probably go. You've given me enough to consider for right now."

Mr. Clark flashed his credit card, and the waiter appeared quickly, taking it from him. "We don't have a lot of time here, Rayne. What do you think?"

"I think I'm going to need at least a couple of days before I can decide."

He inhaled deeply, giving Rayne the sense he was disappointed.

"I'm afraid I can only give you one. You see, we've waited a few weeks for you as it is, and we have a big project that needs to move forward. With or without you." With his chin ducked, he studied her from beneath thick brows. "I'll be waiting for your answer tomorrow evening."

❧

Rayne felt as if she practically stumbled out of the elevator as it opened onto the FountainTech floor. She'd forgotten her laptop, leaving it in her office in her rush to escape her frustration with Jack, with the difficult schedule, yet again with Harold for not promoting her, and finally with Barb. Didn't the woman have any sense of self-respect?

At least it was ten at night, and she didn't have to worry about running into another employee. Everyone was burned out and ready to leave as soon as they could these last couple of weeks. She fumbled with her office door and, finally entering, flipped on the lights and flopped into her chair.

One day. She had one day to decide. Jack would be furious with her.

An image of Jack smiling down at Barb, who had effectively situated herself to reveal her ample bosom, flashed in Rayne's mind.

"Ugh!" Rayne threw a file at the wall. It slid down, spilling papers across the floor.

She sagged in the chair. Since when had she become a violent person? What was happening to her? This thing with Jack was turning her into a monster. A monster who couldn't work. Who couldn't produce the magic fountains that everyone expected.

Even Simon had noticed. She'd stood in the conference room this afternoon, pointing at all the little touches she'd added to make the fountain sing, but did it? She claimed it had, but it was as if she were in a poorly remade rendition of *The Emperor's New Clothes*.

There were no clothes, and only one person was brave enough to stand up to the truth. In this case, Simon had been all too happy to point out that nothing Rayne had added to the water sculpture had made it special.

Jack hadn't said a word. He believed in her. And since he believed in her—maybe even loved her—could she in good conscience desert him in the middle of this project?

Desert him when he claimed he needed her to make FountainTech the best it could be?

A little voice whispered that he said those same things to Barb. Rayne stared at the ceiling, unwilling to listen. She didn't believe that for a minute. Or at least, she didn't want to believe it.

Rayne and Jack—they had something special; they'd connected in a way that couples rarely found. Or was she fooling herself? Was it all part of her overactive imagination?

Her father would certainly say so. What words of wisdom would he give her for this moment? For a minute, she wished she were sitting at the kitchen table at her parents' farmhouse, listening to her father complain about the weather or lecture her about the best method to harvest wheat.

She could hear him now, giving her the advice she longed to hear.

Don't count your chickens—no, that seemed too cliché even for her father. Rayne exhaled loudly, wondering why his proverbs couldn't come to her when she actually *needed* them.

Something was amiss on her desk and drew her attention from her thoughts. Her laptop wasn't in her office. Could she actually have been that stupid? That distracted?

"Oh come on," she said, frustrated for leaving her laptop in the conference room. Hopefully, it was still there.

The halls remained lit during all hours, and Rayne was thankful for that as she made her way to the conference room. Through the glass doors, Rayne could see her laptop still resting on the table. She wished someone had thought to bring it to her office. Everyone was probably too beat to notice or care, the same as Rayne.

She shoved through the doors, relieved they weren't locked, and grabbed the laptop, then left. Harold spoke in hushed but agitated tones from his office, and she found herself involuntarily creeping past, as though she had something to hide.

Did she? She'd just finished dining with Carvis Clark, of a somewhat competitive company, though he'd claimed they weren't in direct competition.

Oh Jack. . .what should I do? She knew exactly what Jack would say, should she bring it up. But wasn't he only thinking of himself and his career? Why shouldn't she do the same?

How was she to make a decision when she felt so torn? *Lord, could you please, this one time, show me what to do?* She squeezed her eyes shut, marveling that she'd gone from wondering if she should have taken this job or stayed on the farm where she belonged, according to her father, to wondering if she should keep this job or move on to the next.

When she opened her eyes, she glanced over her shoulder

and saw Harold peering at her from the doorway of his office.

His eyes narrowed.

⋅❧⋅

Jack stared at the water pump resting on his dining table. Pulling resources from the local hardware store and a few items special ordered on eBay, he'd been able to jury-rig the basic concept behind his pump design—a powerful but streamlined pumping system.

He wanted to enjoy this moment and reflected that Harold had seemed intrigued with his schematics. After quitting EI to free himself from seeing Kiera every day, Jack had worked to come up with a new idea for the next six months, and had even considered starting his own company. That's when he'd gotten the call that FountainTech wanted to talk to him.

Jack only had to couple Rayne's creativity with the latest in technology, and companies would stand in line to acquire a unique water sculpture design created by the exclusive FountainTech, Incorporated.

Harold mentioned using the new design in their bid for the next contract, but Jack was anxious to test it first. The only problem was—Jack slid a chair back from the table and slumped onto it—he'd hurt Rayne. No matter how he'd tried to convince himself that it was for the best, he couldn't get the look on her face out of his mind.

He'd caught her dismay when she'd rushed from the conference room this afternoon. An ache pumped against his ribs—how had he allowed her to leave, allowed his attention to be pulled away by the likes of Barb? In his own defense, he reminded himself that Barb worked under him, too, that she had wanted to share her ideas with him, and he was obligated to listen.

Yeah, right.

Jack kicked the leg of the table, regretting he'd ever allowed himself to grow close enough to Rayne to kiss her. She didn't deserve to be hurt by a cad like him. His stupidity could cost the company as well.

He tapped his cell phone against the edge of the table. Should he call her? Or should he not? For too long already he'd deluded himself into thinking that he could have it both ways—he could pursue Rayne romantically and continue to work with her while she injected the creative spark into the fountains.

Together, Jack and Rayne would create the most spectacular designs the world had ever seen while they explored their feelings for each other. In the meantime, they would ignore the conflict in the workplace their office romance would inevitably cause. All the sticky situations, the jealousy and favoritism that others would point out.

Uh-huh. They'd only attempted to make this work for a short two weeks, and already things had failed miserably. He pictured a fountain when the power had been cut, gurgling and sputtering until it died.

The only way they could be together, really, was if Jack gave up his dreams for FountainTech, for his life, to make something of himself this time.

If he could be sure where things would lead, if he could be sure that Rayne would end up loving him—would he be willing to give it all up for her? Wasn't she worth that?

He smiled to himself a little, remembering how it felt to kiss her. Bolting from the chair, he headed for the fridge to get a soda to wet his dry mouth.

But things were too new, too fresh, for him to know that yet. Weren't they? Jack dialed Rayne's number. He needed to hear her voice. When the call went through to her voice mail, Jack scrambled to think of something coherent to say.

What would he say? After ignoring you at work today, I miss you? The voice mail signaled for him to leave a message. Jack hung up.

❧

Jack woke the next morning, groggy and running late. Not the way he liked to begin his day. He called Carl to let him know how sorry he was that he'd missed their racquetball date. Lately, he thought the game was all that was keeping him sane. It didn't require conversation or too much thought. Instead, it was about reflexes and raw power, slamming the ball as hard and fast as he could, and an opponent who could give as good as he got.

After a quick shower, Jack dressed, tucked his pump securely in the trunk of his car so he could test it in the lab this evening, and headed to FountainTech. He phoned Gail on his way to ask her to order pizza again for a working lunch and let his team know to assemble in the conference room again.

"I've got to put you on hold for a minute," Gail said, and then the expected elevator music resounded through the Bluetooth in his car.

He clenched his teeth. He didn't have time for this.

While he waited for Gail to return, a knot thickened in his throat. Was he focused on work, or was this just his way of seeing Rayne, but in a crowd and from a distance? She would have known he'd called last night, regardless of the fact he'd not left a message.

Why hadn't she called him back?

He supposed he was destined to remain a moron forever. As he raced around the corner to FountainTech, he spotted a large cross on the church located a few blocks down. Sure, he knew it was there and had seen it a hundred times since moving to Fargo, but for some reason, today, he *really* noticed it.

Why now, he wondered? He'd attended Heidi's church a few times, but that was mostly to make friends, and if he was honest, to see Rayne, though she'd never shown up.

Because God had ignored Jack's pain, was Jack ignoring God? Hardening his heart?

He frowned at the idea as he whizzed into the parking garage.

"Okay, Jack, sorry about that." Gail came back on the line. "Something's up."

"What are you talking about?"

"Well, there's some buzz around the office already," she said then lowered her voice so that he could barely understand her. "You need to head straight to Harold's office when you get here. Not sure you want me to assemble your team in the conference room. That's all I'm saying. Oops, gotta go."

She hung up.

Jack clenched his jaw as he rolled into his parking spot. Grabbing his cell, briefcase, and coat, he jumped from the car, carrying his coat over his arm. The days were getting warmer, and he'd just have to tug it off again anyway.

Finally, he stepped from the elevator onto FountainTech's floor and rushed through the glass double doors into the reception area. Gail was on the phone, and with wide eyes, she shrugged at him as he passed, as if to assure him she didn't know what was going on.

Jack hated being in the dark and had the fleeting thought that he should have called Barb to find out what she knew, but, of course, that would be a mistake.

Barb!

He was supposed to meet with her this morning at seven. His chant, "Jack is back," slapped him in the face. He practically trotted down the hallway, dashing past a few members of his team who looked at him warily.

What was going on? He shoved through the door of his office and found Barb sitting there, waiting. She appeared flustered. Unusual for her.

Jack threw his coat over his chair. "I'm terribly sorry that I'm late. I'm afraid I can't meet with you this morning. Something's come up."

"Oh? What is it?" she asked.

He didn't dare look at her but unfolded his laptop on his desk and drew in a calming breath. *I don't know, and if I did, I wouldn't share it with you.* But then again, Barb probably already knew. Jack resisted the temptation to ask if she did.

When he looked through his schedule for the day, ignoring her, she finally broke the silence.

"Well, let me know when you're ready to hear my ideas. I'll be waiting."

Without looking up from his computer, Jack called after her, "Okay, will do."

"Jack." Gail stuck her head in the doorway that Barb had left open.

He glanced up to see her expression. With her head, she gestured toward Harold's office. "Uh, yeah, I'm on my way," Jack said.

Jack swiped his sweaty palms against his slacks. When had he ever been this nervous? And he didn't even know why he was supposed to rush to see Harold. It was probably nothing. Maybe even good news.

As Jack strode the hallways, he injected positive thoughts into his mind. Harold had good news for him. All Gail had said was that something was up. Could be something good, right?

He tapped on the door and stepped inside, shutting the door behind him without being asked.

"Jack, glad you could make it."

Jack gave a half grin at Harold's sarcasm. "Sorry I'm late. What's up?" Why did he have to be late today, when Harold of all people would notice? And Jack was *never* late.

"We have a situation with one of our employees."

"Yeah?" Okay, so this wasn't good news after all. Was Harold referring to Jack's dreaming of a relationship with Rayne that he hoped no one knew about yet? "What kind of situation?"

"I'm afraid our star creator, Rayne Flemming, is fraternizing with the competition. You'll need to terminate her immediately."

Stunned, Jack stared at Harold. *Oh Rayne, you didn't.* "So, what company? You can't blame Rayne if someone is trying to recruit her. That doesn't mean she's accepting a position with them. Let me talk to her. We'll convince her to stay with us." Why would Harold want to fire her over that? After all, Jack came from a competitive company himself, though he'd quit because of a romance gone bad long before hiring on at FountainTech. But still. . .

Harold raised his hand to silence Jack. "It's much more serious than that, son."

Son? So Harold was calling him "son" now? Jack drew in a breath and shrugged. "What then?"

"She's selling company secrets."

Harold had to be mistaken. The ache behind Jack's rib cage suddenly ramped up like it was fueled by a jet engine. He had to throw Rayne a lifeline somehow. What could he say in her defense? "What secrets?"

Because, really, how secret were their secrets once the fountains were out there for anyone to look at?

"Namely, your new pump design. The schematic you left with me was stolen from my office. Then someone saw Rayne with Carvis Clark last night."

eighteen

Jack stared out the window of his office, hardly recalling how he made it from Harold's office to his own.

He'd worried, needlessly, about hurting Rayne.

However, he'd been correct to worry about getting hurt himself. He'd been right to decide he never wanted to love again. Why hadn't he abided by that rule?

Jack thought he'd successfully hardened his heart against the pain, but Rayne had managed to inflict a new kind of pain on him—betrayal. With it came the realization of just how much he cared for her.

He thought he could avoid feeling the pain of loss again, having successfully shoved away the memories of his parents dying in the house fire and recently shoving aside what he thought was love for Kiera.

Falling for Rayne—and he realized now, that he had fallen hard—opened his eyes to the fact that what he had with Kiera wasn't love at all. How could it be love when he hadn't known the real Kiera? But clearly, Rayne wasn't who Jack had imagined her to be either, and she hadn't cared about him. Just like Kiera hadn't cared about him.

He'd prided himself in being able to read people. Was he doomed to lose when it came to love?

The sting of Rayne's duplicity overwhelmed him, drowning him in misery.

Both his office phone and his cell continued to ring, and although someone knocked on his door, he'd locked it and remained unresponsive.

Maybe that's why he'd noticed that cross this morning. God was mocking him, knowing full well what news waited for him. Until this moment, Jack hadn't fully understood what was required to protect his heart. If he'd done a good job, he wouldn't feel this gut-wrenching pain inside. And now he'd do what was needed to freeze his heart. Everything inside him would need to congeal, and soon. Harold expected Jack to fire Rayne.

He closed his eyes and drew on the anger that lingered in the shadows of his heart, anger created from a hundred frustrations—Kiera for starters, and then there was God, who allowed his parents to die. And finally, yes, that was it. . . Jack drew in a breath and fanned to life his fury at Rayne for what she'd done to him.

That was the only way he would survive this moment.

She'd duped him. Finally, when he thought he would explode with rage, Jack composed himself and lifted the phone, dialing Gail.

"Yes, Jack?"

In a calm, flat voice, he said, "Send Rayne to my office, please."

He hung up the phone and stared at the door, remembering he needed to unlock it. In a few short moments, a woman he had been ready to give up his career and dreams for, a woman who had used and duped him, who had sold his design to the highest bidder—might as well have been his soul—would walk through the door of his office.

Jack noticed that he was squeezing the arms of his chair, his knuckles white, so he relaxed his hands, only to see they were trembling. Perhaps if Harold had known how Jack felt about Rayne, he wouldn't have assigned him this task. Then again, had Harold known, Jack could be implicated as well.

A new concern flooded his thoughts. If someone found out about him and Rayne, might he be accused? Though it was Jack's design, Harold could possibly terminate Jack, too, and try to keep the design. Contracts always included the clause that anything the employee created relating to the company while in its employ belonged to the company. Fortunately, because Jack had been working on a design beforehand, he'd negotiated on that point with Harold before joining FountainTech.

Someone tapped on the door, and Rayne stuck her head in. "You wanted to see me?"

"Please, have a seat."

He watched her shut the door and drop into the chair across from him. There were shadows under her eyes, and she looked more fatigued than he'd ever seen her. She must be all too aware that her game was up.

Emotion flooded her expression, filled her eyes. "What's wrong, Jack?"

For an instant, he thought she might reach across the desk, closing the distance between them. Jack imagined quitting FountainTech and leaving with Rayne. They could be together.

A vise gripped his chest and squeezed his throat. That's all he wanted—for them to be together. Finally, he shut his eyes.

But, no, Rayne had used him.

❧

Rayne held her breath. She had never seen this look of complete desperation on Jack's face. And she thought *she'd* had a tough time making a decision—torn about taking an opportunity with another company that would allow her and Jack to be open about their relationship. She'd prayed all night long for a sign from God. Surely He would frown on a relationship that she had to hide. But to go to another company? It reeked of disloyalty.

If she'd learned anything from her father, it was to remain loyal, no matter the cost. And that's why it was so difficult to seemingly turn her back on her parents as she pursued her career and dreams.

She'd call Mr. Clark this morning and given him her answer—she wouldn't be leaving Jack or FountainTech.

As she looked at Jack, the room felt like all the oxygen had been sucked out. Jack's face was lined and pale. His rigid frown deepened, and there was a sadness in his eyes that she'd never seen before. In anyone.

Suddenly, all of those emotions vanished, and his face grew stern, his eyes freezing over. She sucked in a breath. "Jack, please, you have to tell me what's wrong. What's happened?"

Did Jack have family somewhere who had been in an accident, or worse—died?

Jack drew his gaze from hers, and for that instant, his eyes seemed to reflect the tears of a thousand fountains. He toyed with his smartphone, tapping it against the desk.

Clearly, he was searching for the right words.

Whatever it was obviously involved her. An image flashed in her mind, and the room began to spin. "Oh no, Jack. Has something happened to my father?"

His stern expression infused with concern. "What? Of course, not," he snapped, his words harsher than she'd ever heard. Softer, this time, he said, "No, Rayne, no."

"Then what?"

"How could you do it?"

Rayne's jaw dropped open, as she tried to form words. "Oh. . ."

"Oh? That's all you have to say?"

Obviously, someone had seen her meeting with Carvis Clark. "Listen, it's not what it looks like."

"You steal the schematics for my pump and sell them to another company. Tell me how that's a misunderstanding."

The walls tilted again as the blast of his words exploded through her, piercing her like shrapnel. "Wha—?"

"As of this moment, you're terminated." A deep frown lined Jack's forehead, and he rocked his chair around to face the back of the office.

How could he believe she'd do a thing like that? Stunned, Rayne could barely stand, much less voice, the thoughts igniting in her mind in her own defense. Of all the reasons she'd imagined he wanted to see her this morning, something like this hadn't occurred to her.

Regardless that she was being terminated under false pretenses—well, partially false, because FountainTech wouldn't want an employee who was fraternizing with its competition for any reason—she could no longer work with Jack. Not after this. Not after he had believed a complete lie about her and, and. . .

Fired her!

As tears blurred her vision, Rayne knew one thing. God had answered last night's prayers for direction quickly this time.

nineteen

Jack stared out his window, willing himself to remain composed and in control of the situation, willing Rayne to just. . .leave. He watched the clouds gather.

The tension in his office felt statically charged, one wrong move from either of them and the room might explode in white light.

Rayne sniffled behind him. "How could you believe such a thing, Jack?" she asked, her voice barely audible.

Her words sliced him open, severing the last of his control. How was he supposed to endure this anguish? He squeezed his eyes shut, *God, help me. . .*

Jack whirled his chair around to face Rayne, but she'd left without another word. His office door stood open. He grabbed his coat and rushed out and through the reception area. He had to get out of there, get some air.

"I'll be back after lunch," he said, answering Gail's questioning gaze as he shoved through the glass doors.

In his car, Jack pulled out of the parking garage and into traffic. How he wished he could just drive until all his frustrations were spent. Once out of Fargo, he found himself on a lone stretch of highway, and then he passed the little country church where Heidi attended, Rayne supposedly attended, and he'd visited a few times. Fargo Community Church. He recalled his earlier thoughts this morning when he'd noticed the cross on the church he passed on his way into work.

Pain throbbed in his chest, an emotional pain so powerful it had become physical—something Jack had never experienced before. And it scared him. After looking both ways, he made a U-turn and zipped back toward the church, then drove into the parking lot, stopping the car in a marked space farthest from the front door.

Leaving the engine running, Jack pressed his forehead against the steering wheel. What was going on? *Lord, what am I doing here?*

Maybe it was a last desperate attempt to get God's attention because God had ignored Jack and his anguish for far too long. He considered that he should go inside the church and sit in a pew or maybe kneel at the altar if they had one—was there an altar inside the church? Jack couldn't remember. All he knew was that the grief had paralyzed him. He flat out could not move, and if he could, he was sure he would collapse to his knees.

Thump, thump, thump. Jack startled at the sound, bolting upright to see Pastor Luke standing next to his car, knocking on the window.

"Are you okay?" Pastor Luke said despite the fact Jack hadn't lowered the window.

Jack did just that and forced a smile. "Sure, I'm fine."

"I'm not convinced." Pastor Luke lifted a brow. "Why don't you come in, and we'll talk."

Jack shook his head. "No, I couldn't bother you."

"Come on, son. You and I both know that you're here for a reason. Could it be that God brought you here?"

Jack pressed his back against the seat and exhaled slowly. Maybe, finally, God had seen the agony Jack carried. Maybe now God was ready to talk. "All right. You win. I've got a few minutes to spare."

Jack cringed, his last words hitting him squarely in the gut. Could it be all this time that God had been there, waiting on him? Could it be that Jack was the one ignoring God, only giving Him "a few minutes to spare," which rarely happened, if ever?

"Don't worry. You might not have much time, but God has all the time in the world for the perfecting of the saints."

Jack climbed from the car and slammed the door behind

him. Pastor Luke squeezed his shoulder and led him into the little church. Jack took in the pulpit and the stained glass windows, but they did nothing to ease his soul. Pastor Luke then entered his office, Jack on his heels.

"Now, tell me what's bothering you."

Sitting in the chair across from Pastor Luke's desk, Jack stared down at his hands. "I don't have a clue where to start."

How did one go about sharing things like this with a complete stranger, though he was a pastor, a shepherd to the members of this church?

"I should have suggested we pray first, I'm sorry," Pastor Luke said. He bowed his head and began thanking the Lord for all His blessings. Then he moved into praying earnestly for Jack, that God knew his heart and was even now working in Jack's life.

The words disturbed Jack, but probably because they were closer to the truth than he wanted the pastor to know. He hated the moisture surfacing in his eyes, but with it came the lifting of a weight, a washing away of his burdens.

Jack opened up then to Pastor Luke, and to God, as he'd never done before. All of the hurts and frustrations that had occurred in his life, the pain that had left him scarred, seemed to gush out of a deep well. It surprised Jack that he had so much pent up inside him. At times his words sounded harsh and cutting, even to his own ears.

To his credit, Pastor Luke just listened with a concerned but caring look. Jack could see nothing judgmental in the man's expression. When Jack finished, Pastor Luke asked if they could pray again.

"Son, only God can heal these wounds. He's more than willing, but you have to let go of them and give them to Him. I believe you've done that today here with me and with our heavenly Father listening. He's right here, too. Pray again with me, and let's give Him these burdens. They're too much for you to carry."

So Jack prayed with Pastor Luke, and for the first time in

years, he forgave and was forgiven. He hadn't realized the weight he'd carried in his heart. Now he almost felt as if he was floating—spiritually speaking, of course.

"Because God has given us free will, much of the turmoil in our lives is caused by our own decisions and, unfortunately, the decisions of others around us. You can't blame God for your hurts, but you can thank Him now for using this situation to bring you to your knees." Pastor Luke chuckled. "Pun intended. God is in the business of making beauty from ashes."

Feeling like a man newly freed from prison, Jack wished Pastor Luke well and assured him he would call in a couple of days. Walking to his car, Jack noticed he had a bounce in his step that hadn't been there in a while.

The sun broke through the clouds and shined on his car, and at that moment, Jack wondered why he'd so easily believed the news Harold had shared with him about Rayne. He hadn't even questioned the accusations.

⁂

Taking a deep breath, Rayne opened the front door. "Hello, Mom, Dad. Anybody here?"

In the middle of the day, her father was probably in the fields, planting his crop. Rayne headed to the kitchen and almost collided with her mother.

Her mother gripped her arms. "Rayne! What a surprise."

Rayne smiled, still wearing her sunglasses to hide her eyes. "Hi, Mom. Sorry I startled you."

"I was just about to throw together a casserole for this evening. What brings you here in the middle of the week?" She tugged on an apron.

Rayne found a glass in the cabinet and poured lemonade from a pitcher on the counter. "I have some time off and wanted to check on Dad."

Her mother gave a wave of her hand then dragged a casserole dish from under the counter. "You know your father—he's back to work like nothing happened. We've got a farm to run, Rayne. Don't forget that."

Relaxing a little because her mother wasn't scrutinizing her, Rayne shoved the sunglasses onto her head. She took a few swallows of the lemonade then set down the glass. This was it, then. God had finally answered her prayer for direction, and now she'd be moving back to the farm. Her family needed her, and evidently FountainTech did not.

But it wasn't by her choice, and she felt like a failure. Worst of all—

Rayne leaned against the counter for support as she pushed an image of Jack's face from her mind.

How had she even made it all the way out to the farm?

"Honey, are you all right?" Her mother wrapped an arm around her waist. "You sit down here."

Rayne felt herself being guided to the kitchen table and into a chair. This wasn't how she wanted to look in front of her mother. The last thing she needed right now was to have to answer questions. How could she tell her mother that she'd been fired, and that Jack had believed the worst and been the one to do the deed?

"Are you feeling ill? Is that why you came home?" Her mother held her palm against Rayne's forehead.

Rayne leaned her head out of her mother's reach. "I've already told you I came home to see how Daddy was doing." Nausea began to spin in her stomach, and she pressed her hand against her waist. "But you're right. Must be something I ate."

"Well, let's see." Her mother put one hand on her hip and a finger to her mouth. "I've got some Pepto-Bismol in the bathroom upstairs."

"You finish your casserole. I'll lie down for a little while." Rayne forced a smile, though weak, hoping to reassure her mother.

At the bottom of the stairs, Rayne's gaze followed the steps up to the door to her room. Why had she come back? She'd not even stopped at her apartment to pack, and she'd asked

Gail to pack her office things up and ship them to her at the farm. She never wanted to step foot in FountainTech again.

Rayne trembled. No. She couldn't go to her room, because right now she could hardly think straight. She knew that it would only make her feel as if she'd been imprisoned. She thought of all she'd had to overcome to leave this place. Even though she loved the farm, loved her parents, she'd wanted more, and now she was thrown back into the middle of it.

What she needed most was to find solace in the same place she'd always found inspiration. The problem was that place only served to remind her of Jack now.

The front door swooshed open, and Paul rushed in without knocking, just like he owned the place.

Something must have happened. Dad!

"Is it my father? What's wrong?"

His eyes grew wide as he drew in a breath. "No, Rayne, it's you. Are you all right?"

Confused, she shrugged. "Of course, why would you think—"

"Because. . ." Paul glanced around the house. "Let's talk in private."

Rayne wanted to tell Paul no, but how could she? He didn't deserve to be treated poorly. No matter that her life had been shattered today.

"What is it?" she asked.

He tugged her out the door, and she willed herself to follow him over to his truck.

He touched her shoulder. "Rayne, I sent you flowers at your work today."

Rayne didn't think she had any blood left in her face. Her knees went weak, but she clung to the truck door with all her might, still unwilling to admit anything to Paul.

The Adam's apple in his throat bobbed up and down. "Is it true, Rayne? Have you come back to us? They told me you no longer worked at FountainTech."

"They *told* you that?"

"The flower people called me to say they tried to deliver the flowers. When you didn't answer your cell, I called the company directly. The woman there wanted the address to the farm. Said you wanted your stuff sent there."

This day could not get any worse. Rayne rubbed her hands down her face. "Okay, Paul. You cannot tell a soul. I'm not ready to tell anyone. I don't know what I'm doing yet either."

Paul looked hurt, confused. "What do you mean?"

It was ironic. Her parents hadn't believed in her when she wanted to pursue this career. And now Jack didn't believe in her. But Paul. . .

"You've never stopped believing in me, have you?"

A slow smile eased onto his lips. "Or that you'd come back."

Rayne thought he might squeeze her, swing her around in a circle, and then kiss her. That's what made the moment all the more awkward. "Paul, there's something I have to tell you."

twenty

He should have relied on his instinct about Rayne instead of taking Harold at his word.

Lord, this is a new thing for me, asking You for help. But, please, show me what to do.

Using the Bluetooth in his car, he called the office. Gail answered, "FountainTech. How may I direct your call?"

"Gail, it's Jack. I need to speak with Harold."

"Harold's in a meeting. He's not taking any calls."

Jack pressed the gas pedal, accelerating. What could be more important than what Jack had to talk to him about? "Can you tell him that it's me? I'm sure he'll want to talk to me."

"Okay, Jack. Give me a sec."

Fields zoomed past, littered with huge commercial farm tractors, as Jack raced down the lone North Dakota road, waiting for Harold to come on the line.

"I'm sorry, Jack," Gail said. "He's not responding. I'll let him know as soon as I can that you need to speak to him. Is everything okay?"

"Everything is fine, why?" Jack wanted to know what she'd heard about this morning's incident.

"When Rayne left this morning, she asked that I pack her office up and send her things to her family's farm." Her voice trembled.

Jack blew out a long breath he was certain Gail didn't miss. What could he say? At least now he knew his suspicions had been right. When Rayne hadn't been at her apartment, Jack headed toward the farm.

"There's something else. It's probably not important. I just. . ." Gail definitely sounded like she was going to cry. "I had to reject a beautiful bouquet of roses this morning. They were for Rayne."

Oh boy. That *Paul* again.

And Jack? He was nothing but a cad. While Paul was sending her flowers, Jack was firing her.

Though Jack certainly didn't blame him, and it only fueled Jack to keep trying himself.

"Thanks for letting me know. I have an appointment and will be out of the office."

And he did have an appointment. With Rayne.

I hope. He also hoped that before seeing Rayne he would be able to solve the mystery of who passed on a company secret—Jack's new design. Unfortunately, he knew exactly who to call next.

A woman who doubled as a shark and knew industry secrets that slipped past others.

A woman he once thought he'd loved.

He laid off the accelerator. What was worse, her cell number was still in his phone, that is, if she hadn't changed it. Using voice commands, he called Kiera, though he seriously doubted she would answer. But he had to try.

She answered after the second ring. "Jack? This can't be you," she said, in a mocking tone.

He grinned. She'd answered, after all.

"Kiera." It felt funny, saying her name out loud again. At one time he loved the sound of her name. Not any longer.

"I never thought I'd hear from you again."

And Jack was certain she never wanted to either, but that was beside the point. "How are things?"

Her laugh was incredulous. "I'm engaged, now. I suppose I shouldn't even have answered."

"Whoever he is, he's a lucky guy. Congratulations." Surprisingly, the news didn't sting. In fact, it might make this conversation easier. Jack needed to quickly steer this discussion away from their personal lives, though, or things would take a dive—as though they could go any lower. "Listen, I didn't call to talk about our personal lives. Let's talk shop."

"Oh, I get it. Your new job not working out?"

"As a matter of fact, I might be looking." Jack cringed, but truthfully, wasn't everyone always looking for a better opportunity? And right now, yes, he was definitely digging.

"Ah, and you think they might want you back here. Well, I for one will not put in a good word for you if that's what you're asking."

Oh man. This wasn't going as he wanted it to. No wonder he wasn't a lawyer. He couldn't play good cop–bad cop either. Jack did not want to do this, but he was going to have to beg. *Okay, here goes.* "Kiera, I'm sorry that everything between us went sour."

He drew in a breath. *I could use a little help here, Lord.* "And I apologize for every nasty thing I ever did or said to you." There. Actually, that did feel better. "I wish. . .and I wish. . ."

What? Memories of the good times, though few, he'd shared with Kiera drifted over his heart. No. He couldn't possibly wish that he and Kiera were back together because. . .because. . .

He was in love with Rayne.

There, he'd admitted it. And it felt wonderful.

Yes! He pumped his fist.

Except—Jack exhaled long and hard, feeling a deep ache creep back in—he'd just fired the woman he loved.

"Oh. . .Jack." Kiera sounded softer now, oozing femininity. "I've waited so long to hear you say that. I made a mistake."

Say what? Oh no, what had he said? "Kiera, wait. What I mean to say is that though things didn't work out for us, you've obviously moved on, and there's someone in my life who is special, too."

There. He hoped she felt like she had the upper hand again, though he'd almost just blown it.

She sighed.

He knew that sound. Jack cut her off before she could turn nasty. "I want us to be friends, Kiera. Good friends. We don't have to be angry with each other, do we? Especially since you've found someone better than me."

And oh, he'd found someone so much better for him than

Kiera. *Please, God, let me win Rayne back.*

"Oh all right, Jack. Truce. Let's be friends. So, why did you really call?"

"Carvis is trying to steal one of my employees."

"Jack, you know I can't say anything about that. I don't think she took the job anyway."

Really? Jack wasn't sure if that was a good thing or not—because Rayne had reasoned they could be more romantically engaged if she were to work elsewhere—but that was beside the point. Where did he go from here?

"I'm not sure he needed her anyway. He got his hands on something else."

Bingo. Jack froze. "What did you say? Who did he get the drawing from?"

"I don't think I said the word *drawing*. Come on, I've said enough already."

"Look, Kiera, I don't care about the design. I need to know who he got the design from."

"I can't believe I'm talking to you about this. But I don't know anything anyway."

"Can you do this one thing for me? Find out who passed on the design?"

"You could always make me talk, you know that? And now, what are you doing? Trying to get me fired so you can take my job?"

"For old time's sake and because we're friends now."

"How important is it?" her voice grew stern and demanding.

Dread coursed through him. She could very well use this to stab him in the back. But he had no choice. "There's nothing more important to me."

"Really."

He had never liked the Kiera he was hearing now. He bit his tongue, holding off his own sarcastic reply. *Lord, help me. Give me grace here.*

A memory from a Sunday school class he'd attended as a child slipped to the forefront of his thoughts—his Sunday school teacher speaking softly. *"A gentle answer turns away wrath, but a harsh word stirs up anger."* Although he couldn't remember the scripture reference for the verse, it had to be from Proverbs. That much he knew.

Jack slowly released a breath, feeling any remnants of pent-up anger toward this woman seep away with it.

"I hope this new guy knows how to treat you. I hope he knows what a real gem he has—you're one of the most beautiful women I've ever seen." And he meant that.

"I'm onto you, you know that? But I guess if you're willing to grovel like that, it must be pretty important. I'll see what I can find out then call you back."

Jack released the breath he'd held and grinned. "That's all I can ask, Kiera."

"Yeah, well, that's asking a lot, Jack. You owe me."

"Fair enough."

Jack ended the call and tried to think positive thoughts. While he now believed in Rayne, believed she wouldn't have sold him out, there was still a reason to be uneasy. Kiera could come back with Rayne's name. Still, even if Kiera did, there might be some mistake or someone might be trying to place the blame where it didn't belong.

≈

A cool breeze swept against Rayne's face as she stood at the ledge that allowed her to look over her father's fields—her secret place, as she'd told Jack.

This year had been too wet to plant wheat, so her father was going with corn. But he had to get the soil prepared and the crop planted before mid- to late April or else he'd plant barley or soybeans. The farming thoughts settled her heart. In the distance, she spotted several tractors hauling corn planters behind them. In just over a week, she would be able to see the slender blades emerging from the soil, creating row after row of corn.

Her father was one of the few in North Dakota to use a watering system, but he only used it on corn or potatoes because their revenue was much higher than other crops. If she stuck around, she'd be able to watch the water again. Her spirits sagged at the reminder of FountainTech.

When she was a child, this was not only her secret place, but to her child's heart, it was *sacred*. Here she'd talked to God. Here she'd been inspired to create her drawings that depicted wind flowing over wheat. Here she'd watched her father's water sprinkling system irrigate the cornfields, and she'd fallen in love with the fluidity of water.

What had she been thinking, to bring Jack here of all places?

When she thought about it, the hours she'd spent here, after chores of course, had led her to her job at FountainTech. And now she was back.

She rubbed her sleeve against her eyes and cheeks, wiping away the last of the tears—evidence that she'd failed. Her father had been right—it had been a pipe dream at best.

All his proverbs, all his wisdom, and still he was blind to life outside of his farm. Rayne chided herself for thinking about her father in a negative light. But she couldn't help it. At least she wasn't blind to the fact that pride was eating her up inside—she dreaded, with everything in her, the moment when she would tell her father what happened.

That she was back at the farm after all.

Her parents wouldn't gloat that things had worked out according to their plan and not hers. Nor would they care that she was in her twenties and an independent woman, capable of taking care of herself. An incredulous chuckle escaped. They would, however, expect her to marry Paul when all was said and done. He was one of their kind, and surely Rayne could find it in her heart to love him.

If only that were true. But she'd lost more than her job. She'd lost her heart and had nothing left to give to Paul.

She hoped she had put an end to that line of thinking by telling Paul the truth. She loved someone else. Rayne pressed her hands against her chest and squeezed her eyes against the pain balling once again around her heart, constricting her throat.

Crunching footfalls resounded in the copse of trees behind her. She steeled herself, hoping it wasn't Paul. Her heart grew sad at the thought—he was persistent as a mule, considerate and forgiving to a fault. But she would not, could not, love him. Not like she loved Jack—though she'd been woefully mistaken where Jack was concerned. She couldn't marry someone she didn't love, not after tasting something as powerful as what she felt for Jack.

But that was over now. Drawing in a breath, she prepared to face Paul, or whoever had come to seek her out. She whirled around.

Jack?

And took a step back into air. . .

"Watch out." He reached out and gripped her arm, tugging her away from the ledge.

Rayne was stunned to see him, and she looked down to where his hands still held on to her. Slowly, he released her.

Words and thoughts of anger, hurt, and love were jumbled in her head. She couldn't speak.

"Rayne," he said, in a hoarse whisper.

"How. . .how did you find me?" Her throat hurt, but finally she found her voice. The terrain had been snow-covered when she'd brought him here before.

"Paul brought me."

Paul? Why would he do that? Rayne didn't believe Jack. Feeling more confident, she asked, "Why are you here?"

Jack had the strangest expression on his face—a mixture of hope and fear. "Can you ever forgive me, Rayne? I'm so sorry about what happened. I need a chance to explain. Will you give me that?"

He searched her gaze, his eyes roaming down her face and then back to her eyes as if he hadn't seen her in years. Like a man who. . .

No, he couldn't have any feelings for her. "You fired me,

Jack. You believed. . ." *A lie.* She allowed the anger and hurt to harden her, protect her. He didn't deserve to know the truth if, after all they'd shared, he couldn't believe in her, couldn't defend her, and was more concerned about keeping his precious job. Making a future for himself. "You've got some nerve. All you care about is yourself."

Rayne had never heard herself speak in such a hateful tone. It hurt and yet felt good at the same time. *God, please help me. You brought me to this point. Now show me what to believe.*

Jack's face contorted, apprehension flooding his eyes. "I've been trying to figure out how to tell you everything."

Now she turned her back on him again, afraid to let him see how much he'd hurt her. Never again. "There's nothing more to say. Go back to FountainTech."

"I need a second chance. Please hear me out. After what happened, I went to church and met with Pastor Luke."

Rayne frowned at his words, now compelled to listen. She said nothing, though, and waited for him to continue as she watched the tractors planting corn.

"He helped me work through all the hurt and frustrations I've held on to all these years so I could finally resolve that I blamed God for everything bad that ever happened to me."

Rayne looked at the ground to her right, glimpsing Jack in her peripheral vision. "Go on." She still wasn't sure what this had to do with him firing her.

"This was all part of God's plan, leading me to that church today, Rayne. And now I'm free from a lot of pain I've carried."

Finally, Rayne turned to face him. She shrugged. "So, firing me was all part of God's plan to get you to church?" Rayne gave him an incredulous laugh. "I'm glad you've reestablished your relationship with the Lord, Jack. But what does that have to do with me?" She hated the bite that still lingered in her voice.

"Don't you see, Rayne? I've been avoiding a real relationship with anyone, not just God, for a long time, because I was afraid of being hurt, of being betrayed. When Harold said that you had given the design for my new pump to a competitor, all I could see was betrayal. It wasn't within my DNA, within my power, to think anything else, though I wanted to. With everything in me, I struggled to believe that you could ever do such a thing."

"And yet you did believe that."

"It wasn't until getting right with God that the skies cleared for me, so to speak. I saw with clarity that you couldn't be the culprit. I tried to speak with Harold, but he was in a meeting. I drove directly here."

Rayne wanted to believe Jack, but he'd made that very difficult. "Okay, so you found out who stole your design, and it turned out to be someone else. I'm still not coming back to work." She turned her back to him again.

He only believed in her after he'd learned the truth. Where she came from, that didn't count as trust.

twenty-one

Moron. Jack was fumbling and badly. Rayne wasn't buying.

He fought to retain his composure, though everything in him wanted to melt into the ground like the spring snow.

Lord, give me the words. . . .

"No. That's not it. I haven't found out who sold the fountain pump design."

Rayne's shoulders stiffened. Maybe she would listen now.

"I just know, with everything in my heart, that it wasn't you, because. . ."

Jack couldn't believe it, but Rayne slowly turned to face him, tears brimming in her eyes. Her lips trembled.

"You believe that?" she asked.

Now's the moment to be bold. Jack nodded and took a step closer to her, sliding his hand against her neck, cupping her cheek. "How could I believe the woman I love could do such a thing?"

Her eyes grew wide before she squeezed them shut. "Oh Jack. To believe in me, to trust me like that, despite what it looks like. Well, it means everything."

"Rayne, I love you." Jack studied her face, watching her reaction.

She opened her eyes, and in them he saw the depth of her love in return. He saw what he'd hoped and prayed to see. "Will you forgive me?" he asked.

"Oh Jack. I love you, too. There's nothing to forgive. Now, will you kiss me?"

Jack felt his grin nearly split his face. "Will I *kiss* you?" He covered her lips with his, pouring all the pent-up emotions into it, feeling her heart mingling with his. The world seemed a million miles away.

Then Jack's cell phone chirped in his pocket. Rayne tried to tug free.

"Ignore it," Jack murmured against her lips. He loved the feel of her arms around his neck, especially when she pulled him closer.

What he had with Kiera was nothing compared to this.

Oh. . .*Kiera.*

Jack gently ended the kiss then hugged Rayne to him, whispering in her ear, "I need to see who called."

He tugged the phone from his pocket. "It's Kiera. The call I was expecting."

Rayne had a dreamy smile on her face. "Who's Kiera?"

Jack considered what to say to Rayne. Bringing up that he was trying to find out who had passed on his design was bad enough, given that he'd just shared that he believed in her, regardless. But add to the mix that he'd contacted his ex-fiancé to do it probably wouldn't go over well.

"I'm trying to get to the bottom of things." He winked as he waited for his call to connect, thankful and surprised that he had two reception bars out here.

Kiera answered quickly. "Jack, I have only a second."

"What did you find out?"

"Oh, I'm fine, and how are you?"

Jack surmised that someone was near Kiera that she didn't want listening in. "It's great to hear your voice, Kiera."

"I can barely hear yours. Where are you, anyway?"

"You said you didn't have much time, now give."

"Okay, here's what I've learned." Kiera spoke softly.

Jack had to strain to hear and even stuck his finger in his other ear.

"Carvis just sent an offer letter to a guy named Simon Jeffers. My understanding is that Simon is bringing a design with him. Carvis wanted another creator but went with this Simon guy instead, for obvious reasons."

Jack wanted to curse. He'd only recently started the laborious task of patenting his design, but would that matter if someone were bent on stealing it anyway? All Simon would have to do was change the wording on even a small element of Jack's design to create his own patent. "Thanks for the information, Kiera. It means a lot to me. But Carvis is going to have to face the music. Simon, too."

Harold had already contacted the company's attorney. Jack was beyond relieved that Rayne wasn't involved.

Kiera sighed. "I'm sorry. I know this is a blow to you. This business can be so cutthroat."

Jack certainly didn't need to hear that from Kiera, but he shoved his previous summation of her aside.

Harold had pinned the whole thing on Rayne just because another employee saw her talking to Carvis Clark. She was close enough to Jack and knew about the design. He wondered how Simon found out and if someone else was involved. Barb flitted to his mind—she and Simon were pretty close. But let the lawyers figure that one out.

Jack looked at Rayne and gave her a reassuring smile.

"You asked where Carvis got the design, and I've found that for you. I have to go now, Jack. Don't be a stranger."

And just like that, Kiera ended the call.

Jack sighed, feeling as if a weight had been placed across his shoulders again. He tried to tug Rayne to him, but she refused to budge.

"What's going on, Jack?"

He scratched his head. Where did he begin? "Why would Harold think that you sold my design to the competition just because you were seen talking to Carvis? But then again. . ."

Rayne frowned and looked out over the fields. "Apparently he wanted me gone. But why?"

"You're the company's top creative genius. That wouldn't make sense," he offered. Jack tried again to hold her, and this time she stepped back into his arms. "Simon is going to work for Elemental Innovations. Carvis hired him because he's bringing a new design with him. He obviously hasn't given his resignation letter to Harold yet, because Harold didn't accuse him. I wonder if Simon will even come back to work. Probably too scared." In spite of the situation, Jack allowed a chuckle. "Simon was jealous of you, though. And now he positioned himself to take a job offer meant for you. Now *that* makes sense."

"I don't want to think about it anymore," she said and lifted her chin.

Jack answered her pleading lips, shoving thoughts of FountainTech far away.

With a cry, Rayne tore her lips from his. "I know why. The night I met with Carvis. . ." Rayne offered him a sheepish grin then continued. "I went to the FountainTech offices late to get my laptop, which I'd left in the conference room. Harold was there talking to someone on his phone. He must have thought I overheard something, because he looked like he wanted to skewer me alive. But honestly, since I hadn't heard what he was saying, I didn't think another thing about it."

"Until you kissed me," Jack said and grinned. Then he injected a serious tone into his voice. "That might explain things. He discovered the schematics stolen, saw you in the office late, heard about your meeting with Carvis."

A knot grew firmly in Jack's throat. Where did that leave him then? How could he work for FountainTech now, considering that Harold—though he'd misconstrued the circumstances—had asked Jack to fire Rayne? Considering that Jack had gone through with it?

Footfalls pounded and crunched through the trees until Paul appeared, breathless. "Fire. . .there's a fire at the barn!"

❧

Rayne sat in the center seat of the truck's cab, squished between Paul and Jack, as Paul steered his truck over the unpaved and bumpy road. Her head struck the top of the cab at one point.

But she didn't care. Fear coursed through her at the thought of the house burning. Too many things were crashing down on her at once. As Paul swerved the truck around a bend and onto a better road where he accelerated, Rayne wanted to ask him why he'd brought Jack to see her.

But her thoughts were smothered when she finally saw for herself the plumes of smoke spiraling into the sky. Rayne clasped her hand to her throat. "Lord, please keep my family safe."

At her words, she recalled that Jack had lost his family in a house fire. A quick glance at his face showed her the deep lines there. She reached down and squeezed his hand. He'd called 911 for them because Paul couldn't find his cell phone, and she wondered if it had brought back memories.

He squeezed back and then wrapped his arm around her, pressing her head against his shoulder. "Everything is going to be all right."

"I'm not so sure. We live so far out. I don't even hear the sirens yet." Rayne untangled herself from Jack and gripped the dashboard as Paul yanked the truck into the circular drive behind Jack's sports car.

Flames licked out the top and sides of the barn. "At least it's not the house," Rayne heard herself saying.

Paul, Rayne, and Jack were out of the truck in no time, running to assist her father, who had hooked up a water hose and sprayed the barn. He must have seen the smoke from the fields and come in.

This couldn't be good for him. Rayne's mother just stood there, sobbing, which surprised Rayne. She'd always seen her mother as a strong person. But then again her mother had carried a heavy burden since her father's heart attack. He'd just recently begun working the farm in full force again. Rayne's heart ached to see her mother like this.

Paul stepped forward. "Let me do that, Mr. Flemming."

Rayne's father fought him off. "I can do this."

"Of course you can. I'm just giving you a break."

"Please, Daddy," Rayne offered with a soft smile. Finally, her father relinquished the hose to Paul and stumbled back. Rayne hugged him. "Fire trucks are on their way."

"They won't make it, Rayne."

"We have to think positive; we have to pray."

"Our only hope now is that flames or sparks don't reach the house. I guess we could pray for rain."

Rayne couldn't stand to hear the sound of defeat in her father's voice, but his comment reminded her of when her mother told her about her name. She'd been born during a severe drought, and they'd been praying for rain every day. The day she came into the world, it finally rained. Her mother said she'd been an answer to prayer, so they named her Rayne.

Her mother had then paraphrased a Bible verse from Acts. " 'He has shown kindness by giving us rain from heaven and crops in their seasons; he provides us with plenty of food and fills our hearts with joy.' You are my rain from heaven, child."

Rayne couldn't help but weep at the thought. *Lord, can You send Your rain now? Save my parents' farm? I'm sorry for wanting more when You've already given me so much.*

"Oh honey." Her mother handed her one of the ever-present tissues from her pocket and squeezed her. "Don't cry."

Rayne smiled at her mother, who'd apparently composed herself. This was the strong woman Rayne knew as her mother. *"A strong man is a man who gets back up after he falls."* Her father's words comforted her. Maybe her mother had recalled something that brought her strength as well.

While looking at her mother, understanding washed over Rayne: Despite her mother's plain appearance, through the years it had been her mother's inner strength that had supported them all.

She was the glue that held them together.

"It's going to be all right," her mother said.

"That's just what Jack told me." At the thought, Rayne looked around. "Say, where'd he go?"

Jack wasn't anywhere to be seen. Rayne began to worry. "Jack!"

Though Paul was doing everything humanly possible, the water coming from the hose wasn't nearly enough to dampen the flames. "Paul, have you seen Jack?"

He shook his head, concentrating on focusing the water on the fire. "No! I could use his help, too. We need to spray water over the house, keep it wet in case some embers hit the roof."

"I'll help you with that." Rayne looked at her mother. "Where are the fire trucks?"

Rayne's mother pulled her red-eyed gaze from her husband, her expression somber. Rayne's father looked pale and stricken. "You take care of Daddy. I'll see to everything else."

Her mother nodded her agreement and walked over to Rayne's father. She ushered him toward the house. He looked crushed. How could he give up so easily? Rayne knew that her mother was far more concerned about her father's health than she was about the farm.

Her mother escorted her father through the front door. The fact that he would go so willingly surprised Rayne and could only mean that he wasn't feeling well. *Lord, please let the emergency crews get here quickly.* She didn't even hear any sirens.

Then, to her horror. . .

The wind kicked up, and she watched as an ember from the barn floated across the distance and landed on the roof of the house.

"No! Paul, the house!" Rayne yelled. "Focus on the house."

Where did her father keep another water hose?

Suddenly, it was as if the heavens opened up and dumped rain on all of them. Only it wasn't coming from the sky. Water soared to an incredible height then came tumbling down onto the house, effectively stamping out the ember that had landed on the roof. As the water continued, Rayne felt confident the house would be too wet to catch fire. As the sirens finally sounded in the distance, she wasn't sure the firefighters could top what she was seeing.

But where was the water coming from? She dashed around to the back of the house and found Jack standing next to a pump. He'd apparently tapped into the well pump, going directly to the source for the water, and plugged his pump into the house. Scattered around him were the junk parts from an old wheel line irrigation system her father had attempted to fix.

He grinned at her. "Well, what do you think?"

Relief washed over her. Love for this man flooded her heart. "I think you just saved the day in more ways than one."

❧

That evening, after all the fire crews had left the Flemming home, the scent of smoke and wet ashes lingered in the air.

Crickets chirped, and stars shone brightly in the night sky as though nothing out of the ordinary had happened. As though the barn hadn't burned, or Rayne hadn't lost her job, or Jack hadn't fired her. None of those things seemed to matter now.

Jack smiled at the peace that flooded his thoughts, and continued to rock the swing where he and Rayne nestled on the Flemming porch. He knew she remained overwhelmed with the events of the day, but all he cared about was that she was in his arms.

At last.

They were together. Jack vowed to allow nothing to keep them apart again. Not FountainTech or any other company for that matter, not a farm or parents who wanted her to marry a farmer. Nor would Jack allow his career plans to stand in the way of their happiness.

He chuckled to himself, remembering Paul's lecture as the guy drove him to Rayne's secret place. She'd only imagined it was secret.

"What's so funny?" Rayne asked, her head against his shoulder.

"Would you believe Paul?"

Rayne pulled away from Jack and sat forward, twisting to stare back at him. "How is Paul funny?"

Her hair was crumpled against the side of her head. Jack reached out to run his fingers through it. He could tell she was beyond tired and probably needed rest. But he couldn't bear to let her out of his sight. At least not yet.

"When Paul drove me to find you at your secret place, he gave me a lecture on treating you right, what sort of woman you are, your likes and dislikes. Rayne, the guy loves you."

Rayne sighed, clearly not pleased. "I talked to Paul already about how I feel."

"I know, Rayne. Don't get upset. Paul loves you enough to give you up and even make sure that the man who won your heart won't hurt you. I don't think I could have done the same."

Rayne smiled softly. "You're saying Paul knew that he was bringing you to see me because you love me?"

"Yep."

Rayne frowned. "He'll make some woman a wonderful husband some day."

"Well, since you brought it up. . ." Jack's heart drummed like he was in a rock band. He cleared his throat.

She looked at him, studying his gaze, a question in her eyes. Did she realize he had a question for her? "With everything that's happened today, I haven't found the right time to talk to you."

Come on, man, do this right. Jack feared the timing was all wrong, but he wouldn't leave anything else to chance. Wouldn't let her slip away again. He pushed himself out of the swing then bent down on one knee.

Rayne leaned forward, her hair hanging over her face, but he could see the shy smile on her lips and the reflection of moisture in her eyes. It was all the fuel he needed to proceed.

He placed a hand over his heart. "Rayne Flemming, my soul was dry and cracked until you came into my life and gently watered it, nurturing me back to life. Will you marry me?"

She threw her head back and laughed then gave him a teasing punch. "Some people might think that was corny, but"—she drew near and pressed her forehead to his—"not me. I loved it." Emotion was thick in her throat as she continued. "You know, my family didn't want me to take the job, to pursue my dreams, believing it would tear our family apart. My parents and their parents before them were all farmers. This farm belonged to them. If I left, who would continue on in the same house that has been in the family for generations? Who would farm the land? But in following my dreams, I found you, and you filled a need they could never have anticipated. You saved their home. You saved the farmhouse, Jack."

His knee aching now, he climbed up to sit next to Rayne on the bench, keeping his face near hers. "So, is that a yes?"

Rayne smiled softly and wrapped her arms around his neck, just the way he'd grown to love, tugged him forward and kissed him, long and thoroughly.

He had his answer.

❧

Rayne pressed her head against Jack's chest, cherishing the warmth and love she felt there, floating on the dreamy high produced by his proposal as he brushed his fingers through her hair.

The screen door creaked. "Oh Rayne. I'm sorry to interrupt," her mother said.

Pulled from the moment, Rayne disentangled herself from Jack. "Is everything all right?"

"Yes, it's just that. . .your dad wanted a few words with you."

Rayne stood and looked down at Jack. "You coming?"

He smiled up at her. "I'll wait. You probably need some time alone with you family to deal with the loss of the barn."

"I'll just be a minute." Rayne followed her mother into the den. Surprisingly, her mother had a peaceful expression on her face.

Her father sat forward, his hands clasped between his knees as though he was preparing words for Rayne. She swallowed. She had some news for her parents, too.

How would they take it?

Rayne dropped into the chair next to the sofa where her father waited. Though circles rimmed his eyes, his face was a mixture of pain and joy.

"What's wrong, Dad?"

"Nothing and everything." He slid over to the corner of the sofa and took Rayne's hands in his. "There's something I need to tell you."

"What's wrong?"

He stuck his hand up. "Don't imagine the worst now; just let me say what I have to say."

"Okay." Rayne couldn't remember her father ever speaking to her in this manner. It scared her.

"When I had the heart attack, my mind filled with all manner of thoughts. What would your mother do without me? How would she work the farm? Who would look after you since you're not married?"

Rayne opened her mouth to object, but her father thrust his hand up again. She kept her words to herself.

He seemed to relax a bit, having eased into his spiel, and slid to sit against the sofa back. "When a man has a close call, when he almost dies, he thinks crazy thoughts. I even thought that maybe God would use my heart attack to bring you home to us."

His audacious words astounded Rayne, but she held her tongue, knowing he had more to say.

A moist sheen filled his eyes, and he pursed his lips, waiting until he could speak. Rayne's eyes watered as well, unable to watch her father so near tears.

"Oh Rayne. I've been so arrogant."

Her mother stepped into the room at that moment with a carafe Rayne assumed was coffee. She'd apparently already set a tray of cups and condiments on the coffee table. Rayne hadn't even noticed until that moment. Her mother gave her a soft smile, and Rayne once again focused on her father.

"When the barn caught on fire and I feared we'd lose the house, too, I realized that as important as these things are—they've been in our family for generations—they mean nothing to me compared to you."

"Oh Daddy," Rayne said, her voice trembling through the rush of tears.

"Baby, I've been selfish, refusing to see that God had other plans for you. He gave you this incredible artistic gift, and now I realize He wants you to use it for something special. You've been doing the right thing all along." Her father looked down at his hands as though he feared her reaction.

"What your father is trying to say"—her mother, who'd been leaning against the doorway, now dropped onto the sofa next to Rayne's father and took his hand—"is that with all that's happened, God opened our eyes."

Her father smiled. "And when I saw that water spraying from your boss's pump, saving the house from the embers that traveled from the barn, I saw how special your work is. And it takes strength and character to follow your dreams. You've done that. I couldn't be more proud of you, Rayne."

He stood and tugged Rayne to her feet and into a hug. Unable to help herself, she sobbed, releasing all the pent-up anguish she'd held inside because she wanted—no, needed—her parents' approval.

When her father let her go, he gripped her shoulders and looked gently into her eyes. In his, she saw the approving look she'd been missing for several years now. It felt good and nurtured her thirsty soul.

She swiped at her cheeks. "You have no idea how much it means to me to hear you say this. No idea how important this was to me." And Rayne had no idea until that moment how crushed she'd been, living without their approval.

Her mother hugged her as well.

Rayne stood back and eyed them both. "I've got some news for you, too."

"This wouldn't have anything to do with Jack, would it?" Her father grinned.

twenty-two

The corn stood tall in the fields of the Flemming farm by the time Rayne waited in the foyer of the small church where she would marry Jack.

Only a few minutes and a short bridal march down the aisle separated Rayne from her future husband—a man with a good heart. The sort of heart she'd been waiting for. So what if it happened to be packaged inside an incredibly handsome man? She hadn't been looking for him, but then, she'd heard that was sometimes how a person found his or her spouse.

Heidi had agreed to be Rayne's matron of honor and stepped out of the little room where she'd dressed, revealing her beautiful mauve silk and taffeta dress. When she saw Rayne, she gasped. "You look gorgeous. As in every man's dream gorgeous. Jack is a lucky guy."

Rayne's father lifted her hand to his lips and kissed it. "My little girl getting married. Never thought I'd see the day."

"Oh, of course you did, Daddy." Smiling, she stifled any words regarding her father's previous expectations that she'd marry Paul.

Fortunately, Paul had already found a lovely young woman from a neighboring farm to lavish his attentions on. Rayne had never doubted he would make a wonderful husband but just not for her.

She was more than grateful she hadn't succumbed to the pressure to stay at the farm and marry Paul.

Thank You, Lord.

Moisture brimmed in her father's eyes, surprising Rayne. He squeezed her hand. "I know I've already told you this, Rayne, but I love you, and I've always prayed for you. For

God to give you direction. You looked so lost to me, not seeing where you needed to go. Now I realize it was me all along. I didn't see where you needed to go. Praying for *you* changed *my* heart."

"Oh Daddy." Rayne dabbed at the corner of her wet eyes. "You're going to mess up my makeup."

He grinned. "I want you to know that I couldn't be more proud of you."

Rayne thought she would lose it right there and then as her father pulled her into a gentle hug.

God was so good. Though she'd thought He wasn't answering her prayers for direction, He knew exactly what He was doing—everything worked out in His timing the way that it should.

In a way, Rayne would be returning to the farm. She and Jack had started their own company called Dream Fountains. Though they planned to focus on creating water feature designs, they also agreed to develop water sprinkling systems for farmers that would deliver water more efficiently and be more cost-effective.

Rayne struggled to believe how everything had worked out—for her good and for Jack's. The scripture in Romans gently floated into her heart. *"We know that God causes all things to work together for good to those who love God, to those who are called according to His purpose."*

Suddenly, with the scripture spoken to her heart, Rayne recognized the Holy Spirit's gentle voice—all this time she'd wanted to hear something from the Lord, to know if she was going in the right direction. Now finally she saw that God had been directing her all along. He'd never left her side. Each step she'd taken had been part of the process, and Rayne was called according to His purpose.

Eyes tearing up again, Rayne looked anywhere but at her father. Out the window, autumn leaves had already begun to fall. As the seconds ticked by, Rayne skimmed the small foyer, taking in the plush carpet and the gorgeous flowers in mauve and off-white—her wedding colors—sitting on ornate pedestals. Fargo Community Church had been the place where Jack had found the Truth. God had been ready to listen, and Jack had given Him his pain. Then Jack had believed in Rayne. Rayne had since agreed to join Jack at the small church, attending weekly. She quickly wondered what had taken her so long to join. In addition to enjoying time seeing Heidi and the others, she'd made new friends. They'd all been such a blessing to her. Made her feel welcome and at home at her new church.

Suddenly the sound of the "Wedding March" began, and the double doors gently opened. Rayne stood in the center of the doorway, her heart in her throat as the small gathering stood and turned to face her. Gripping her father's arm, she took the measured steps forward, feeling self-conscious that all eyes were on her.

But when she drew close enough to see into Jack's eyes, the world around her faded. All her thoughts, hopes, and dreams stood before her, wrapped inside a gorgeous, honorable man with a good heart. He was deep-thinking and understood her thoughts before she even spoke.

Together they were like the magic in the water features they created. Before she knew it, she stood across from him, only the splash of wedding colors in her bouquet between them. Looking into Jack's eyes, she repeated the vows, as did he, but she was too nervous to comprehend it all.

Then he was slipping the wedding band onto her finger where it fit snugly in place next to her solitaire diamond engagement ring. Heidi held the bouquet for her.

"I now pronounce you husband and wife. You may kiss the bride," Pastor Luke said, joy in his voice.

Jack took her hands in his and bent, pressing his lips against hers. His kiss was soft and gentle yet held all the power and promise of a glorious future together. Still holding hands, they turned to face the crowd as they were instructed during the rehearsal.

"I'm pleased to present to you, Mr. and Mrs. Jack Kostner."

Jack and Rayne hurried down the steps and across the aisle between the pews to the doorway. Before they could leave for their honeymoon, they planned to remain in the church fellowship hall for a short reception.

Rayne could hardly believe it—she was a married woman. Her father was right when he said, "The higher your aim, the harder your fall."

She'd aimed awfully high when she set her hopes on Jack, deciding that she loved him. In that moment, Jack glanced over at her, his unspoken love apparent in his eyes.

Rayne had fallen very hard, indeed.

ròa

Rayne squinted in the sunshine as she and Jack emerged from a side exit of their elegant hotel in Maui—the perfect place to honeymoon.

Palm trees waved in the salty ocean breeze, and the scent of exotic flowers enveloped Rayne, intoxicating her. The long flight over the Pacific Ocean to Hawaii had left her with jet lag the first couple of days. But now on her third day here, she was feeling like herself again—although newly married, she might never feel like the old Rayne again. But why would she want to?

Jack's love was taking her to places she'd never been before, and she never wanted the adventure to end. He angled his head toward the sun. The sunglasses he wore seemed to enhance his handsome appearance. How she'd ever ended up with such a gorgeous man, Rayne would never know. Still, all good gifts came from the Father above. She grinned.

Her new husband flashed a brilliant smile then bent down, fitting his mouth against hers. She succumbed to a rush of emotions then fought them. "No, no. I want to see Hawaii before we leave. Is that all right with you?"

Jack laughed. She'd never grow tired of hearing that sound.

"There's something else I want you to see," he said. Walking arm in arm, they meandered along the sidewalk, passing families and other couples who looked like they were also in love, until they came to the front of the luxurious hotel and stopped.

She gasped and watched as a choreographed fountain danced to theme of the movie *Australia*. Powerful emotions kept her riveted, for how long, she wasn't sure. It was all she could do to finally speak.

"Oh Jack. It's beautiful." Tears of joy slid down her sun-warmed cheeks.

Seeing a fountain like this, performing full-featured and live, rather than on her laptop or in the mini-lab, stole her breath. She pressed her hand against her heart. While she'd worried over the details of their wedding, Jack had planned their honeymoon, and now she understood why he'd wanted to.

Though difficult, she tugged her gaze from the fluid motion of the water and studied her handsome new husband. In response, he turned his head to her and smiled. He looked like a man without a care in the world. Like a man in love.

Rayne's head swam with the dizzy thoughts of his love.

"Is it your design?" she asked.

"Yes, I created it while at EI."

"Seeing the actual fountain like this, the real thing, I can't find the words."

Jack watched the fountain in silence then faced her again. "Nothing I've ever done can compare with your talent." Jack drew near and whispered against her lips, "Or with you. Rayne, *you* are the real thing for me."

A Letter To Our Readers

Dear Reader:

In order that we might better contribute to your reading enjoyment, we would appreciate your taking a few minutes to respond to the following questions. We welcome your comments and read each form and letter we receive. When completed, please return to the following:

Fiction Editor
Heartsong Presents
PO Box 719
Uhrichsville, Ohio 44683

1. Did you enjoy reading *Praying for Rayne* by Elizabeth Goddard?
   ❏ Very much! I would like to see more books by this author!
   ❏ Moderately. I would have enjoyed it more if

   _____

   _____

   _____

2. Are you a member of **Heartsong Presents**? ❏ Yes ❏ No
   If no, where did you purchase this book? _____

   _____

3. How would you rate, on a scale from 1 (poor) to 5 (superior),
   the cover design? _____

4. On a scale from 1 (poor) to 10 (superior), please rate the
   following elements.

   ____ Heroine   ____ Plot
   ____ Hero   ____ Inspirational theme
   ____ Setting   ____ Secondary characters

5. These characters were special because? _____

_____

_____

6. How has this book inspired your life? _____

_____

_____

7. What settings would you like to see covered in future
   Heartsong Presents books? _____

_____

_____

8. What are some inspirational themes you would like to see
   treated in future books? _____

_____

_____

9. Would you be interested in reading other **Heartsong
   Presents** titles? ❑ Yes ❑ No

10. Please check your age range:

    ❑ Under 18   ❑ 18-24

    ❑ 25-34   ❑ 35-45

    ❑ 46-55   ❑ Over 55

Name _____

Occupation _____

Address _____

City, State, Zip _____

E-mail _____

Heartng

HEARTSONG PRESENTS TITLES AVAILABLE NOW:

___HP685 *Thunder Bay*, B. Loughner
___HP686 *Always a Bridesmaid*, A. Boeshaar
___HP689 *Unforgettable*, J. L. Barton
___HP690 *Heritage*, M. Davis
___HP693 *Dear John*, K. V. Sawyer
___HP694 *Riches of the Heart*, T. Davis
___HP697 *Dear Granny*, P. Griffin
___HP698 *With a Mother's Heart*, J. Livingston
___HP701 *Cry of My Heart*, L. Ford
___HP702 *Never Say Never*, L. N. Dooley
___HP705 *Listening to Her Heart*, J. Livingston
___HP706 *The Dwelling Place*, K. Miller
___HP709 *That Wilder Boy*, K. V. Sawyer
___HP710 *To Love Again*, J. L. Barton
___HP713 *Secondhand Heart*, J. Livingston
___HP714 *Anna's Journey*, N. Toback
___HP717 *Merely Players*, K. Kovach
___HP718 *In His Will*, C. Hake
___HP721 *Through His Grace*, K. Hake
___HP722 *Christmas Mommy*, T. Fowler
___HP725 *By His Hand*, J. Johnson
___HP726 *Promising Angela*, K. V. Sawyer
___HP729 *Bay Hideaway*, B. Loughner
___HP730 *With Open Arms*, J. L. Barton
___HP733 *Safe in His Arms*, T. Davis
___HP734 *Larkspur Dreams*, A. Higman and
        J. A. Thompson
___HP737 *Darcy's Inheritance*, L. Ford
___HP738 *Picket Fence Pursuit*, J. Johnson
___HP741 *The Heart of the Matter*, K. Dykes
___HP742 *Prescription for Love*, A. Boeshaar
___HP745 *Family Reunion*, J. L. Barton
___HP746 *By Love Acquitted*, Y. Lehman
___HP749 *Love by the Yard*, G. Sattler
___HP750 *Except for Grace*, T. Fowler
___HP753 *Long Trail to Love*, P. Griffin
___HP754 *Red Like Crimson*, J. Thompson
___HP757 *Everlasting Love*, L. Ford

___HP758 *Wedded Bliss*, K. Y'Barbo
___HP761 *Double Blessing*, D. Mayne
___HP762 *Photo Op*, L. A. Coleman
___HP765 *Sweet Sugared Love*, P. Griffin
___HP766 *Pursuing the Goal*, J. Johnson
___HP769 *Who Am I?*, L. N. Dooley
___HP770 *And Baby Makes Five*, G. G. Martin
___HP773 *A Matter of Trust*, L. Harris
___HP774 *The Groom Wore Spurs*, J. Livingston
___HP777 *Seasons of Love*, E. Goddard
___HP778 *The Love Song*, J. Thompson
___HP781 *Always Yesterday*, J. Odell
___HP782 *Trespassed Hearts*, L. A. Coleman
___HP785 *If the Dress Fits*, D. Mayne
___HP786 *White as Snow*, J. Thompson
___HP789 *The Bride Wore Coveralls*, D. Ullrick
___HP790 *Garlic and Roses*, G. Martin
___HP793 *Coming Home*, T. Fowler
___HP794 *John's Quest*, C. Dowdy
___HP797 *Building Dreams*, K. Y'Barbo
___HP798 *Courting Disaster*, A. Boeshaar
___HP801 *Picture This*, N. Farrier
___HP802 *In Pursuit of Peace*, J. Johnson
___HP805 *Only Today*, J. Odell
___HP806 *Out of the Blue*, J. Thompson
___HP809 *Suited for Love*, L.A. Coleman
___HP810 *Butterfly Trees*, G. Martin
___HP813 *Castles in the Air*, A. Higman and
        J. A. Thompson
___HP814 *The Preacher Wore a Gun*, J. Livingston
___HP817 *By the Beckoning Sea*, C. G. Page
___HP818 *Buffalo Gal*, M. Connealy
___HP821 *Clueless Cowboy*, M. Connealy
___HP822 *Walk with Me*, B. Melby and C. Wienke
___HP825 *Until Tomorrow*, J. Odell
___HP826 *Milk Money*, C. Dowdy
___HP829 *Leap of Faith*, K. O'Brien
___HP830 *The Bossy Bridegroom*, M. Connealy

(If ordering from this page, please remember to include it with the order form.)

Presents

Great Inspirational Romance at a Great Price!

Heartsong Presents books are inspirational romances in contemporary and historical settings, designed to give you an enjoyable, spirit-lifting reading experience. You can choose wonderfully written titles from some of today's best authors like Wanda E. Brunstetter, Mary Connealy, Susan Page Davis, Cathy Marie Hake, Joyce Livingston, and many others.

When ordering quantities less than six, above titles are $3.99 each.
Not all titles may be available at time of order.